VOICE FOR THE SILENT

Voice For The Silent

…"Dude, you're not a drug dealer, are you?"

He didn't dodge as Juke reached out and stroked a finger down his nose. Chuckling, Juke shook his head. "No, BB. I'm not."

BB nodded, not sure he could speak with as dry as his mouth had suddenly gone. In all his twenty-one years, no one had ever touched him so gently. Not even his mother. Not that his mother had been around much during his life. She'd given birth to him and dumped him on his aunt and uncle before running off with her very own drug dealer.

Before BB's mind adjusted to what had happened, Juke slipped off into the shadows, moving like the predator BB had always assumed he was. He fingered the business card Juke had handed him. He wanted to go back to the kennels, to be there when whatever went down happened, yet he doubted he'd be any help to the dogs.

All his life, he did what he had to do to keep the dogs safe, and none of it mattered. Uncle Caesar continued to fight them. The dogs continued to die, and BB's heart continued to break. Maybe it was time to step back and try to straighten out his own fucked-up life before he did any more for the dogs.

Juke had said Queenie was all right, and, for some reason, BB trusted the man not to lie to him about that. Whoever Juke really was, he seemed to be honorable about that. Some spark of hope burned in BB and he found himself thinking maybe God had finally answered one of his prayers. Maybe the abuse would stop and the dogs would be free to be dogs, though BB knew the odds against the canines were huge.

Being raised in an environment like his wasn't conducive to hopes and dreams. A man survived as best he could and hoped he didn't meet a bloody end at the hands of another human…

ALSO BY BY T. A. CHASE

Air And Dreams
Allergies
Bastet
Be The Air For You
Bitter Creek's Redemption
Duncan's World
Freaks In Love
Lift Your Voice
Nick Of Time
Nowhere Diner: Finding Love
Revealing The Past
Shades Of Dreams
Soothe The Burn
Wolf's Survival

VOICE FOR THE SILENT

BY

T. A. CHASE

AMBER QUILL PRESS, LLC
http://www.amberquill.com

VOICE FOR THE SILENT
AN AMBER QUILL PRESS BOOK

Amber Quill Press, LLC
http://www.amberquill.com

PUBLISHED IN THE UNITED STATES OF AMERICA

Thank you to all my readers who help me get through the day when the writing starts to drive me crazy. Also, thank you to all the animal rescue shelters and volunteers who give unselfishly to help some of God's most innocent creatures from the cruelty of people who should know better.

*"I've been treated so wrong
I've been treated so long
As if I'm becoming untouchable..."*

—"My Skin" by Natalie Merchant

VOICE FOR THE SILENT

CHAPTER 1

The cacophony of noise beat Julio down. He kept his gaze averted from the ring, not wanting to see the sickening sight of dogs tearing into each other. The growls, whimpers, and yelps were nearly drowned out by the yells of the crowd gathered around the ring. Julio tried to wander through, not pushing or giving any of them a reason to remember him.

His little video camera attached to his shirt captured the faces of the bloodthirsty men and women, though he did notice that most of the women looked as disgusted with the whole event as he did. They didn't have much say as to whether they wanted to be there or not. Only the dogs had less control than the women over their lives.

Julio hoped the camera caught some good clear images. It was time to shut down this dog-fighting ring. The men running it were getting suspicious of Julio's constant appearance at the fights, yet he never bet or even stayed the whole night.

His leaving before it was over irritated not only his partner, but his superiors. He couldn't tell them that if he stayed until the conclusion, he'd end up vomiting in the corner or something. It was bad enough he went home and took an hour-long shower, trying to wash his body clean of the violence and blood, even when he hadn't gotten close enough to get dirty. His mind imagined him covered in red.

Julio hadn't gotten a full night's sleep since he started this assignment, and he doubted he would until it was over. The only light in the whole sordid thing was that he'd gathered enough evidence to shut down this ring, though his boss wanted the smoking gun. He wanted Julio to videotape the men killing underperforming dogs or something equally damning. Julio didn't think he could stay there and watch while a monster killed an innocent dog. It went against everything in his nature.

He'd become a police officer to protect the defenseless, and a Humane Society investigator because, hell, there wasn't anything more defenseless than an animal. They had no voice to speak of cruelty or abuse. They had no way of sticking up for themselves. Julio could do it for them, and wanted to with all of his heart.

His team had shut down three dog-fighting rings so far, but this one was going to be the largest bust in the history of the Humane Society. He certainly would be arresting some of the highest profile people. It would be bigger than when that football player got nailed for running a dog-fighting kennel.

"Hey, Juke," a voice spoke from right beside him.

Julio managed not to jump before turning to look at Caesar, one of the leaders of the ring. "Hey, man, how's it going?"

"Good, dude. Real good. Got two grand champions set to fight at the end of the night. Oh, I need you to stay after. I got a proposition for you."

Grimacing inside, he nodded. "Cool. I might have to leave for a few, but I'll be back."

"Sure. No problem." Caesar squeezed his shoulder hard and wandered off to chat up some other guy wearing an Armani suit.

Who the hell wears Armani to a dog fight? Julio shook his head and strolled off toward the exit. Nodding to the men guarding the entrance, he slipped out and headed to where his truck sat far enough way from the lights and people, no one could see him pull out his phone.

"What you got, Herendez?"

"Not much except video of the people at the fights, but the big guy wants me to stay after. Says he has a proposition for me."

"You armed?"

"Yeah. They don't expect a dealer like me to wander around without some protection."

"Good. We're not that far away. If something starts going down, you get the hell out of there and we'll take them. I don't want to lose this case, Herendez."

"Understood, sir."

Julio caught movement out of the corner of his eye. "Hey, gotta go.

Call you later."

He hung up and stuck his phone in his pocket. Reaching around, he eased the gun from the small of his back and carried it close to his leg as he snuck closer to where the darker shadow was.

"Come on, baby. Just a little farther and you can rest." Desperation colored the speaker's voice.

Julio heard a whimper as he inched closer.

"I know you're hurt. That's why we gotta get you out of there. Uncle will kill you. It don't matter to him that you make good pups. He just sees that you can't fight no more. I won't let you die."

Julio was close enough to see a slender youth leading a limping dog from the back of the building. It was obvious every step the dog took was painful, but there wasn't any way the kid could carry it. The youth looked like he'd blow away in a gentle breeze. Slender didn't come close to describing the teen. Not sure why he did, Julio disengaged the camera on his shirt. Something said the kid wasn't a willing participant in the fighting.

A twig broke under Julio's foot and the kid dropped, covering the dog with his body. Looking directly at him, Julio thought how incredibly beautiful the kid was. What moonlight drifted through the trees painted the young man's face with silver, highlighting gorgeous cheekbones and illuminating bright blue eyes.

Surprise and fear welled in those eyes, and Julio discovered he wanted to reassure the kid he wouldn't do anything to him. Of course, how believable was that when he held a gun and, if the kid hung around the fights, he'd seen Julio in his undercover role. Juke, drug dealer and all-around badass.

"BB," Caesar shouted, and the kid gasped.

Realizing he was going to regret this, Julio did the only thing his mind would let him get away with. He gestured for the kid to go.

"I got her," he said softly, moving closer to the pair after tucking his gun in his waistband.

"How do I know you won't just shoot her after I leave?"

The kid had guts; Julio gave him that. Not only did he have to worry about Caesar finding out about him taking the dog, but he was questioning Julio like the man didn't carry a Glock in his waistband and hadn't beat up some asshole for just looking at him wrong.

"You have to trust me, kid. I'll get her out of here." Julio reached out and gave BB a push. "Now go, or he'll come out here and there's no way we'll be able to save her."

"BB, you fucking asshole, where are you? I need you in here." Caesar's voice ripped through the night, causing BB to jerk in terror.

"Go."

Julio didn't wait for BB to move. He swooped in, snatched up the dog, and carried her quickly to his truck. After setting her down, he opened the door and managed to get her in without hurting her worse. At least, he hoped he didn't do any more damage. The dog didn't make a sound, not even growling at him, though she had to be in a lot of pain. Maybe she knew he wouldn't hurt her, or maybe she had lost enough blood, she just didn't care what happened to her.

He stroked a hand over her wide head before stepping back and looking down at his shirt. *Shit.* There were dark streaks on it, which could only be blood. Quickly, he dug through one of his duffle bags and pulled out a clean shirt that was an exact match for the one he wore. After changing them out and switching the camera to the new shirt, he patted the dog one more time and tossed a blanket over her. It would keep her warm. He didn't worry about anyone looking in. The windows were tinted so dark no one could see into the vehicle.

He strolled back inside, nodding to the guard before wandering closer to the ring. There was a lull in the action, and Julio knew it meant the big fight was coming. Two grand champions were slated to fight that night. One was Caesar's own male, Stu. Julio cringed every time he saw the dog. Stu's face and chest were covered with scars. At times, it seemed like it hurt for Stu to walk or do much of anything, but his overwhelming need to please his owners drove the dog to fight, even when he couldn't move.

The dogs were brought to the ring, and Julio allowed the rush of the crowd to push him out of the way. He'd gotten enough video of the fights, he didn't have to stay around for those. He eased his way through toward the back of the building, where the handlers usually hung around when their dogs weren't fighting. Julio kept his eyes open for BB. Something about the kid called to him.

It had been a long time since Julio allowed himself to feel any sort of attraction. Yeah, he figured BB was underage—and didn't that make him feel like a perv?—but he couldn't stop thinking about him.

What kind of courage did the kid have that he'd be willing to risk Caesar's wrath by sneaking a wounded dog out of the building? Knowing Caesar as well as Julio did, he wouldn't doubt if the man discovered the kid doing that, Caesar would kill BB where he stood. No one went against the big man.

The sound of flesh hitting flesh caught his attention, and Julio casually walked down past the cages of dogs. Some of the animals lay in their cages quietly, overwhelmed by the scents of fear and anger. Others barked or whimpered, wanting to run away, but trapped in the wire boxes that held them until it was their time for blood and violence.

"I don't want to."

BB's voice drifted to Julio's ear and he moved closer to one of the remaining stalls in the old barn. It was far enough away from the city not to draw attention, and the owner of the property turned a blind eye to what happened there as long as the money was good.

Staying in the shadows, he peered into the stall and saw Caesar, BB, and another older guy. Blood trickled from a split lip on BB's face, but Julio saw disgust and more fear in the kid's eyes.

"I don't give a shit if you want to or not, BB. This man's paid me good money, so you're gonna do what he wants. You know what'll happen if you don't."

Caesar gestured to the corner and Julio saw a small brindle pup cowering away from the men. *Fuck!* Something told Julio threatening the dog would get BB to do anything Caesar wanted.

Defeat settled on BB's shoulders and he pushed away from the corner to walk toward the older guy. Julio didn't like the way the man studied BB, like the kid was a walking piece of meat he planned on devouring.

None of your business, Julio. You're here for the dogs. Take care of the ring and the kid gets free.

Why didn't that make Julio feel better? His thoughts made him careless and he kicked one of the cages, giving the dog inside a reason to lunge at him.

"Who the hell's there?"

Caesar stalked out to find Julio muttering into his phone. He looked up at the bald, overweight white man and held up a finger.

"All right, *puta.* I'll be there in a few minutes. You tell that asshole he don't get nothing until I talk to him. He's screwed me out of too much money."

He flipped his phone shut and kicked the wooden stall door in anger. Caesar eyed him suspiciously.

"Sorry, *hermano.* It sucks being a businessman these days, huh? Can't get good help. They don't stay off the shit." Julio shook his head. "So the fight's about to start. Thought you'd maybe like to watch it with me and give me some pointers on what makes a good fighter. I'm thinking about starting my own kennel."

Caesar stared at him for a moment before breaking out into a big smile. "Great idea. I've got a couple pups I could sell you."

Julio looked over Caesar's shoulder for a quick second, catching BB's questioning gaze. The other man wasn't looking at them; he was visually fucking BB where he stood. Julio nodded slightly, knowing BB understood what he was saying, while Caesar thought Julio was agreeing with him.

Some of the tension left BB, but Julio knew BB was still going to have a hell of a night before it was over. He let Caesar drag him off to discuss the finer points of dog-fighting, while Julio tried not to think about what the stranger was doing to BB.

Somehow, he made it through the last fight of the night without losing his mind or the contents of his stomach. When Stu stood, victorious, over his fallen opponent, Julio looked into the dog's eyes and saw no blood lust or rage. No, Julio saw anguish and helplessness. This particular dog didn't want to fight. It wasn't bred into him through centuries of selective breeding. No, he'd been trained to fight and knew nothing else, and unfortunately for him, that meant attacking and even killing his fellow canines. Before the handlers closed in, Stu dropped his head and nuzzled the dog, seeming to be saying he was sorry. It broke Julio's heart.

* * *

BB closed his eyes, ignoring the grunting sounds coming from behind him, and trying to block out the burning of his ass while the stranger fucked him. He'd gotten good at it. It always confused him that men who would have killed a gay man didn't seem to have a problem fucking him. What made them straight if they were screwing another guy, even if they had a woman at home? Though he doubted most gay men would force another to have sex with them.

Maybe that was it. It wasn't so much that the men who fucked him were gay. They just liked the idea of having BB at their mercy. He didn't have a choice about it. He had to let them have his body or the dogs would suffer. He couldn't allow that. They already were hurt so much, he couldn't knowingly allow them to endure more pain because he was a coward.

At least Queenie got away or, at least, he hoped she got away. Juke seemed willing to help him earlier and had signaled to BB that the dog was fine. BB wasn't big on praying since God had never really seemed to answer any of his pleas before, but he prayed Juke would take care of her. He didn't want to think the drug dealer could've lied to him and had either turned Queenie back over to his uncle or was keeping her to start his own kennel.

God, get this over with quickly.

Yet BB knew it wouldn't be the end of it. Uncle told him the stranger had paid for a full night with BB and that meant just because the man came this time, BB was stuck there until the man sent him home or the sun rose. BB had no idea what time it was. All he could do was pray his buyer got bored with him soon.

He had dogs to take care of. That was his job after the fights. He was the one to nurse the winners back to health, while he tried not to think about the losers. There would be empty cages when he got back to his uncle's and the knowledge made his heart hurt.

"That's a good boy. I'm coming."

Christ's sake, just do it! BB screamed silently, needing it to be all over.

One more hard slam into him that shoved BB's head into the wall at the front of the bed. He whimpered at the newest pain, but the guy fucking him chuckled and patted his ass.

"I knew you enjoyed this. You look like a cocksucker. I should have you blow me after I take a nap." The man grunted and froze, his cock deep inside BB's ass. With a deep groan, he came. "Oh, fuck, yeah."

BB's phone rang as the guy was sliding out of him. He lunged for it, wanting to answer it, but also to get away from the bastard on the bed.

"Yeah?"

"Get your ass back here."

"But…" He protested simply to do it, not because of any real wish to stay at the hotel. He grabbed his jeans from the floor and tugged them on.

"Don't question me, boy. Just do it." Caesar hung up.

BB frowned. What had put the desperation in his uncle's voice? It was an emotion he'd never heard from Caesar before.

"Where are you going?" The man reached out and grabbed BB's wrist.

"I have to go. My uncle wants me back at the kennels."

The man sat up, sweat glistening on his pasty white skin. His flaccid cock still covered by the rubber lay limply on his thigh. BB swallowed hard, trying to think about something other than what had just happened. If he did think about it, he just might break down, and he couldn't do that yet. Someday, when he and the dogs were safe, he'd crumble into a broken pile of heartache, but today wasn't that day.

"What the hell? I got you for the entire night. That's what your uncle and I agreed on."

"You'll have to take it up with Uncle Caesar. I'm sure you can work out something else with him." BB jerked his hand free, snatched up his keys, and raced from the room.

No way was he staying there any longer. Not when he had his uncle's permission to leave. He headed to his beat-up truck and unlocked the door. Before he could climb in, he was grabbed from behind and dragged into the shadows by the side of the hotel. He kicked and fought, but screaming was useless because of the hand covering his mouth.

"BB, settle down. It's me, Juke."

BB froze, sure he heard that wrong, but the slightly accented voice whispering in his ear was familiar. He'd heard it several times before talking to the dealer earlier that night. He struggled to turn around, and Juke let him.

He stared up into the man's dark eyes and swallowed. "What are you doing here?"

"I followed you after the fight."

Oh, God! Embarrassment swamped BB and he ducked his head, letting his hair block Juke's view of his face. The dealer knew what was going on. There wasn't any way he didn't know Caesar had sold BB to that guy.

What did it matter what Juke thought of BB? The dude sold drugs for a living and got his jollies watching dogs tear each other apart for sport. What kind of man would do that? No, Juke was just another monster like his uncle. Yet BB didn't remember ever seeing Juke stay all night at one of the fights, except tonight. He shook his head. Didn't mean anything. No one cared about BB or the dogs. He had to deal with all of it on his own.

"What'd ya want? Uncle called. I gotta get back to his place." He crossed his arms over his chest and glared at Juke.

Juke checked around the corner before he faced BB again. He scrubbed his hand over his dark hair. BB tried not to stare at the tattoo that danced on Juke's cheek just below his eye. He knew what that

10

small black teardrop meant and it didn't fill BB with confidence.

"Don't go back to his place, BB. It's not going to be safe for you there."

BB snorted. "What makes tonight"—he looked up at the lightening night sky— "or I should say today any different? That place ain't been safe for me in years."

Juke huffed out a low breath. "Trust me, kid. You don't want to be there when the shit hits the fan."

"I ain't a kid." He didn't know why he said that. It wasn't any of Juke's business how old he was.

"Fine. I don't give a shit how old you are. Just don't go home right now. Some shit's going down in the next couple of hours, and you don't want to get caught up in it." Juke stuffed his hands in his front pockets like he was trying to keep from touching BB.

"Why should I trust you? Where would I go? I got no place else. No other family than my uncle. You think if I did, I'd be living with him, letting him do this shit to me?"

The way Juke eyed him made him nervous. It was like the guy peered into BB's soul and saw all the dreams he'd buried deeper each year.

"Actually, I think you stay because of the dogs, kid. You could've run away a long time ago." Juke pulled something from his pocket and handed it to BB. "If you need a place, call this number and tell the person who answers Julio told you to call. They'll give you a place to crash. No questions asked. Nothing owed."

"Julio?"

Juke's laugh was harsh and low. "Do you seriously think my mama called me Juke?"

Okay. The man had a point.

"Fine. I'll call and go there, but what's gonna happen to Uncle Caesar? How do you know?" BB fidgeted as his nerves started zinging. "It's got something to do with the dogs, don't it? Damn, man, I can't let anything happen to those dogs. It's not their fault my uncle's a bastard."

"True, kid. Don't worry about the dogs. They'll be safe soon enough." A beep came from Juke's phone and he pulled it out to look at the screen. "I've got to go, BB. Please, just call that number. Oh, and Queenie's going to be okay."

Relief rippled through him at that knowledge. "Can I see her?"

"Once this all blows through, I'll get a hold of you and take you to her. How's that?"

"Dude, you're not a drug dealer, are you?"

He didn't dodge as Juke reached out and stroked a finger down his nose. Chuckling, Juke shook his head. "No, BB. I'm not."

BB nodded, not sure he could speak with as dry as his mouth had suddenly gone. In all his twenty-one years, no one had ever touched him so gently. Not even his mother. Not that his mother had been around much during his life. She'd given birth to him and dumped him on his aunt and uncle before running off with her very own drug dealer.

Before BB's mind adjusted to what had happened, Juke slipped off into the shadows, moving like the predator BB had always assumed he was. He fingered the business card Juke had handed him. He wanted to go back to the kennels, to be there when whatever went down happened, yet he doubted he'd be any help to the dogs.

All his life, he did what he had to do to keep the dogs safe, and none of it mattered. Uncle Caesar continued to fight them. The dogs continued to die, and BB's heart continued to break. Maybe it was time to step back and try to straighten out his own fucked-up life before he did any more for the dogs.

Juke had said Queenie was all right, and, for some reason, BB trusted the man not to lie to him about that. Whoever Juke really was, he seemed to be honorable about that. Some spark of hope burned in BB and he found himself thinking maybe God had finally answered one of his prayers. Maybe the abuse would stop and the dogs would be free to be dogs, though BB knew the odds against the canines were huge.

Being raised in an environment like his wasn't conducive to hopes and dreams. A man survived as best he could and hoped he didn't meet a bloody end at the hands of another human. He'd done what he had and lived to see twenty-one. At one time, he'd never believed he'd grow that old.

The sun rose and BB looked down at the card. There was a phone number on it, but no name or anything else. Pulling out his phone, he flipped it open and started punching in numbers, trying not to let his fears change his mind.

He moved to the corner of the building and canvassed the parking lot before heading to his truck. He climbed in and locked the door behind him while he waited for someone to answer.

"Yeah?"

"Julio told me to call you." BB's voice shook a little as he spoke.

"Write down this address. I assume you're coming right now."

"I can't go home. Or at least, that's what Julio said."

"Okay." The man rattled off an address and had BB repeat it back to him. "Where are you at?"

BB told him, and the man grunted.

"So you're about thirty minutes away. I'll have things ready for you when you get here." The man went silent for a second. "I know you have no reason to believe this, but you can trust me and Julio. Neither one of us is looking to hurt you."

BB couldn't say he really believed the man, yet he was willing to give it a try. Right at that moment, he wanted someplace he could wash the grime and stink of the ring and the hotel off him before sleeping for several hours.

He should be worried about his uncle, but he couldn't dredge up any concern. Whatever happened to Uncle Caesar was the man's own damn fault. The dogs were all BB cared about and he understood that he might not be enough to save them.

"I trust Juke, man. I'll be there in thirty."

"The door will be open."

BB started the truck and drove away, praying that his life would be different soon.

CHAPTER 2

Excited tension filled the air as Julio put his vest on and checked his gun. He slipped his badge over his neck, letting it hang down over his chest. The other agents around him were getting ready to serve the warrant on Caesar Addison's kennel property.

His boss had looked at the last video Julio had brought in and decided they were to go in the next morning. Emerson had taken their evidence to the DA, after which they headed to a judge to get the warrant signed.

"Where'd you go?"

Julio looked up to see Smith, one of his fellow agents, approach him. "I had to take care of some business. Has anyone heard from Emerson yet?"

"No." Smith tugged on his own vest. "He'll be here soon."

"I hope so." Julio's phone vibrated in his pocket. "I've got to get this."

"Fine." Smith wandered away to talk to some of the other waiting agents.

He pulled his phone out and answered it. "Herendez."

"*Hermano*, what did you send me?"

"Pedro, did he get to your place?" He moved off, not wanting the others to hear him.

"Yeah, he's upstairs taking a shower now." Pedro grunted. "Who is he? Another stray you picked up?"

"I can't really talk right now. BB's part of a case I'm working on. I

14

didn't want him going back home. That's why I gave him your number. Thanks for taking him in. I appreciate it."

"You'd do the same for me." Pedro laughed. "In fact, you have done the same for me. Is he a rent boy like I was?"

"Not by choice, I'm afraid." Julio braced his shoulder on a tree in the park they were gearing up at. "I'm getting ready to arrest his uncle, who sold him to other guys."

Pedro swore. "Shit. That sucks, bro. Well, with Santo gone, I can take him in for a while."

"Thanks, man. I'm not sure when I'll be able to get over there. Just keep an eye on him and see if he's okay. Let me know if he needs anything. This case is going nuclear soon, and I'm going to be knee-deep in reports."

"Herendez."

Julio stood and nodded at Smith. "I have to go. Take care of BB and yourself, Pedro. Remember to call me if you need anything."

"Will do. Be safe, Julio. You're the best friend Santo and me ever had."

After hanging up, Julio stuffed the phone back in his pocket and went to join the other agents as they gathered around Emerson, who'd just pulled up.

"Got the warrant. SWAT is heading over to secure the property now. We need to saddle up and head out, everyone."

They all double-checked their equipment before hopping into their vehicles. Julio rode with Smith and two of the others.

"Herendez, you the one who broke this case?" one of the other agents asked.

"Yes. I went undercover as a dealer. Ended up going to several fights."

"How was that? I've never seen one in person. I can barely watch the videos," Smith admitted.

Julio swallowed and said, "Horrifying. There were times I had to leave and go throw up without anyone seeing me. Doesn't look good when a big, bad dealer gets sick from watching dogs rip each other apart."

The guys laughed, but not in a bad way. They seemed to understand why Julio had such problems.

"I don't know how you do it. This will be the third ring you've busted, right?" The other guy sounded impressed.

"For some reason, I'm good at what I do." Julio rubbed his finger over the tear-shaped tattoo at the corner of his eye.

Smith looked at him out of the corner of his eye. "I think you're dedicated to your job and you love animals. It pisses you off when people take advantage of the innocent."

"It could be."

They pulled up in front of the small trailer Caesar used as his headquarters for his kennels. The SWAT team had already secured the trailer and gestured to the Humane Society officers. Julio headed toward the back where the dogs were chained. There were at least ten dogs tied up outside; their chains were heavy and solid logging chains. It wasn't surprising, since dog fighters liked to use those steel chains to help the dogs build up their muscles.

There were two pole barns, and Julio entered the first one. The noise swelled as the dogs barked. None of them lunged aggressively at him. They pawed at their cage doors or tugged at their leads. Julio found Stu, Caesar's big stud dog. Stu had his own big kennel with a run that led outdoors. The black pit bull sat down and studied Julio as he approached the cage door.

When Julio crouched down by the door, Stu didn't move closer, but didn't cower either. It was obvious the dog didn't trust Julio, yet he wasn't afraid of him either. Julio gestured to one of the agents.

"This is Stu, a grand champion. Be careful when you take him out of here. It doesn't look like he'll be violent, but it doesn't hurt to be careful. Don't hurt him or yourself."

The agent nodded, and Julio made his way out of the building. He wanted to search the second building. It was important to find equipment of fight training. One of the SWAT team guys came up to help him open the locked door of the second barn.

Once the door was ajar, Julio flicked on his flashlight to look for a switch. The windows were painted black and sealed shut. There was a string hanging down and Julio yanked on it. A bare bulb flooded the room and Julio grinned. *Bingo!*

He looked at the SWAT guy. "Can you go and send some of the agents in here?"

Tugging out the gloves he carried in his back pocket, Julio walked around the entire area, just looking at everything. There was a treadmill and more chains. On one of the tables were several bottles. Julio picked one up and read the label.

"Steroids," he muttered softly.

After setting it back where he found it, he wandered over to where four short walls had been set up into a makeshift ring. There were dark splatters along the sides and Julio figured if someone did a test, they would find out it was blood.

"What have you got, Herendez?"

Julio turned to see his boss stalk through the doorway. "I've got training equipment. A training ring. Some steroids and other drugs to bulk the dogs up. There's probably blood on this wood."

He gestured to where some wires and knifes hung.

"Test that stuff and you'll find blood on those as well. I believe Caesar and his associates used those to kill dogs that didn't work out." Julio bit his lip and swallowed his nausea. "I didn't see any of it, but Caesar told me about getting rid of the dogs that wouldn't fight or were too injured to fight anymore."

"Yeah. We got some of that on tape." Emerson growled before waving to the other agents coming in behind him. "Take pictures and box everything. We need all of the evidence we can get. Now if only we can find the dead dogs. That would be the smoking gun for sure."

Julio grimaced, but said, "I might have a way to find those. I need to make a phone call."

Emerson eyed him for a few minutes and nodded. "Go make your call. I'll get things moving in here."

Pushing through the crowd, he made his way outside and to the edge of the clearing where some dogs were housed. The dogs whined at him as he took off his gloves and yanked out his phone. He dialed Pedro's number and waited for his friend to answer. Crouching down, he held out his hand to a little white dog that cringed away from him, but wagged its tail. Yeah, there didn't seem to be any viciousness in the dogs, just fear. But fear could be just as dangerous if not treated carefully.

"What do you want?" Pedro's voice came over the phone holding a smile in the words.

"I need to talk to BB. Can you get him to the phone?"

"Sure, man."

Pedro set the phone down, and Julio heard muffled voices before the receiver was picked up.

"Hello?" BB's voice was hesitant and slightly fearful.

"Hey, BB, this is Juke. I need to ask you something." He hoped the younger man would be willing to tell him the truth.

"Go ahead. Don't mean I'll give you the answer."

At least he seemed honest.

"Okay. I need to know if there are any dead dogs buried on Caesar's kennel property and if there are, where the gravesites would be?"

Silence reigned for several minutes. Julio fought the urge to ask if BB was still there. He could hear the man breathing into the phone.

"Yes, there are. Uncle Caesar killed about ten of them and maybe about three others died because I couldn't take care of their injuries." BB's voice wavered.

"I'm sorry." It wasn't enough, but it was all Julio could offer at the moment.

"Yeah, so am I." BB took a deep breath. "If you go out past the training barn, there's a trail there. Go about a half-mile into the woods; you'll find another clearing. That's where I buried them. Did the best I could for them, but it weren't enough."

Julio shot a look over his shoulder and noticed no one was around him. "Don't worry about them anymore, BB. Your uncle's going to jail and will be there for a long time."

"Has he been arrested yet?"

"Not sure, but there were agents going to his house around the time we raided his kennel. He should be in custody as we speak."

BB grunted. "I should be there. Not just for the dogs."

"Herendez, get your ass back here," Emerson shouted.

"I have to go. You don't need to be here, BB. We've got things covered and the dogs will be taken to a shelter where they'll be very well taken care of."

"You won't kill any of them, will you? They don't deserve to be killed because of my asshole uncle." BB's words sounded watery, like the man was fighting back tears.

Julio stood and headed back toward the training barn. "I promise none of them will be put down. Well, if I have anything to say about it. They seem like good dogs. You did a good job caring for them, BB."

"But I couldn't keep them from fighting or dying." BB hung up on him.

True, and it was a guilt every person held because so many people turned their backs on the grim reality of dog-fighting rings. Calling BB back and telling him he wasn't to blame crossed Julio's mind, but Emerson grabbed his arm and dragged him closer.

"Did you find out where those dead dogs are?"

"Yes, sir." He led the way around the outside to where the trail was. "If we follow this out about a half-mile, there's a clearing where the dogs were buried. There should be thirteen bodies there. Ten killed. Three died from wounds received while fighting."

Emerson whirled around to yell for diggers and the vet. Turning back to him, Emerson ordered, "You lead them to the graves. Make sure all protocol is followed. I don't want this bastard to get cut loose because of a fucking loophole or mistake."

"Yes, Captain."

Julio didn't want to go dig up the dead dogs. He didn't want to know how they were killed, yet he knew it was his job to find out those things as much as he hated the knowledge.

Thirty minutes later, one of the shovels hit something soft. They all looked at each other, knowing that the worst part of the job was about to be revealed. Two agents dropped into the pit and started scraping the dirt away, while others got the body bags ready.

Julio stood a few feet away, manning the video camera. He tried not to shake or move in any way, but the thought of how much pain those dogs had suffered during their lives hit him hard. He gave himself a mental shake. Enough of that. There would be time later to mourn the dogs and wallow in rage for everything Caesar had done.

His time now had to be focused on gathering the evidence that would send Caesar to jail and ruin the man's life. It wasn't just a vendetta against Caesar. Julio felt the same way about any person who thought hurting an innocent made him more of a man.

* * *

Standing, BB stared at the phone he'd just turned off. Christ, they were raiding his uncle's kennel and house. What if they took the girls away? Katie and Betsy wouldn't do well in a house that wasn't their own. He admitted it was strange considering how the girls were used to going home with other men.

Should he have asked Julio about the girls? He didn't want to bother the man and he didn't have Julio's number. Julio was in the middle of dismantling Uncle Caesar's business of pain and terror. BB had no family loyalty to the Addisons, even though he carried the last name. His mother might have been an Addison, but Uncle Caesar and Aunt Daisy never made him feel like a part of the group. Not that being a part meant anything special, considering what his uncle did to his own daughters.

"Julio get what he want?"

BB set the phone down and turned to see Pedro stroll into the room. "Yes." He cleared his throat. "Does he do this often?"

"Do what?" Pedro glanced at him while picking some dishes off the coffee table.

"Send you strangers to house and not tell you anything about them." BB shrugged. "I could be a dangerous person, looking to steal what I can."

Pedro snorted. "Trust me. Julio wouldn't have sent you to me if he thought you'd be dangerous to me. Of course, I can take care of myself. I spent some time on the streets, BB. I have an idea what's been going on with you."

Dropping his gaze to his dirty tennis shoes, he blushed. He didn't want other people to know what he'd been doing. Maybe if it had been his idea he wouldn't be nearly as embarrassed, but being forced to do it changed his outlook.

He rolled his eyes. Not like most people would choose to sell their bodies, but still by making it his own choice, it would have given him power over it. What had brought Pedro to the streets? The slender, dark-haired man seemed to be in control of his life. He had a nice house and, from the pictures, a gorgeous boyfriend.

"I know that it looks like I'm talking through my ass." Pedro gestured to the nice furniture and big room. "But trust me, there was a time when I didn't know where the fuck I was going to sleep from night to night. You know, I'm gay."

BB looked pointedly at one of the pictures on the fireplace mantel showing Pedro in the arms of a tall man. He could see the love between them in their smiles and the way they stood with each other.

"Okay, I don't hide it. Well, at least, not in my own home. I tend to be a little more discreet in my public life." Pedro nodded with his head toward the kitchen. "You want a cup of coffee or some breakfast?"

He didn't, but he didn't want to go to sleep. He followed Pedro into the other room and sat down while Pedro took out some bowls and a box of cereal from the cupboard.

"Sorry. I don't have time to make anything. I have to get out of here to get to work on time."

"This is more than I usually have for breakfast."

"What do you usually have?"

BB poured cereal into the bowl and added milk. "Nothing. My uncle didn't really think I needed to eat very often. Sometimes, I'd just be coming back home from being out all night."

"Hmmm…I remember those days. Glad I don't have to do it anymore." Pedro chewed for a second before saying, "You know you can do something different."

"Not like I chose to do it."

The bitterness in his voice must have alerted Pedro to how he was feeling.

"Well, maybe not, but you can walk a different path now because there won't be anyone around to hold you back." Pedro stirred his cereal. "Plus, you'll have Julio backing you. He'll support you and won't let you get down on yourself."

"How long have you known him?" BB found himself curious about the man who had saved him and Queenie.

"About six years now. Met him his first year on the force. That's the regular police, not the Humane Society investigation branch." Pedro stood and rinsed his bowl out. "He helped me and my boyfriend. I took you in because I owe him and I trust him. He wouldn't send you to me if he thought you'd do something to me."

BB stared at the flakes in his milk. "He must know me better than I know myself."

Pedro paused and looked out the window. "At times, I think Julio understands people better than he knows. He's got an ability to read people and see what's inside them. I mean, you'd like to do something else with your life, right? You don't want to become whatever your uncle is or was."

"Hell, no. I never want to be anything like him."

"Then Julio was right about offering you a way out. My advice: don't screw it up. Do all you can to make yourself a better person."

"I don't have any money."

"There are ways to do it and agencies that'll help you without money." Pedro checked his watch. "I have to go. You're welcome to crash in the guest bedroom. Do you need some clothes?"

BB shook his head. "No. I got my backpack and a change of clothes in there."

"Okay. I'll see you later on today then. I'm usually home by five. We can find something for dinner when I get home."

"Where's your boyfriend? Won't he get upset you let someone stay without consulting him?"

Pedro chuckled. "Santo is out of the country at the moment, and I think he's secretly in love with Julio, so what ever Julio wants, Santo's fine with it."

"Don't that worry you?"

"What? That Santo's in love with Julio?" Pedro winked. "No. Santo and I have been together for a long time. I know him. He might have a crush on Julio, but he wouldn't do anything about it. Also, Julio wouldn't either. Julio's an honest guy. Wouldn't break up a couple."

"At least he has some morals," BB mumbled.

Pedro left the room, and BB went after him into the living room. He watched Pedro slip on a suit coat and pick up a briefcase. BB didn't say anything when Pedro walked out of the house.

After the door shut, BB made his way upstairs and found the bedroom Pedro had pointed out to him. He stripped out of his clothes and dropped them on the floor before he climbed under the blankets.

BB punched his pillow until it was just right for him. He stared at the blank white wall across the room from him. He'd gotten used to sleeping during the day when he didn't have the dogs to care for. What would he do now the dogs didn't need him anymore? They would go to a shelter somewhere and others would take care of them.

He already missed all of them, especially Stu and Queenie. All the dogs had meant something to him, but those two held a special spot in his heart. Maybe the dogs would finally be allowed to be dogs instead of fighting machines.

CHAPTER 3

The barking and whimpering threatened to drive Julio over the edge. There wasn't anger in the noises, though. This time there was fear and worry. The dogs didn't understand what was going on. All they knew was they were in a different place where they slept on cement and lived indoors. There wasn't any place to run and no way to see any of the other dogs they'd lived with all of their lives.

He wandered up and down the aisles of the shelter in the area big enough to take all of Caesar's fighting dogs. In a way, Julio was glad they were still together. Stopping in front of one of the kennels, he leaned against the wire door and gazed at the dog occupying it.

Stu stared back at him. There wasn't any aggression in the black dog's eyes, just simple bewilderment. Stu didn't understand any of what was going on. His tail thumped softly on the floor, and Julio crouched down to make himself look less threatening.

"You're a good dog, Stu. I'm not going to let them do anything to you. Not a chance."

Public outcry poured in as soon as the media got hold of the news about the bust. The biggest dog-fighting ring in the country had been broken up and there were sixty dogs looking for justice. Oh, a majority of the people swore the dogs were vicious and should be put down immediately. There was no way to rehabilitate fighting dogs. They were dangerous creatures, just waiting to turn on humans or other dogs.

Julio didn't believe that. He'd never believed it, even before meeting these dogs. Hell, Queenie had been living at his house for a week and she'd never once showed any inclination to attack his other two dogs. She'd recovered nicely from her injuries, and Julio had fallen in love with her.

His superiors didn't know Queenie existed, and Julio was going to keep it that way. He wasn't going to allow the sweet dog to go into the system, especially a system disinclined to give her a second chance.

While he thought about the dogs, Stu moved closer and lay down next to him. Julio reached through the wire and stroked his hand over Stu's muscular back.

"I know someone who'd love to see you," Julio murmured.

BB was safe, but Julio had chosen to stay away from the young man. He didn't want to bring the kid into the investigation unless he had to do so. Plus he wasn't entirely sure BB realized Julio was the one who brought his uncle's business down and he didn't know how the guy would react to that.

"Back again." Renee, one of the shelter volunteers, joined him in front of Stu's kennel.

"I can't seem to stay away." He pushed slowly to his feet, not wanting to startle Stu. "I've got a ton of evidence to sift through, along with witness testimony to take down, yet every free minute I have, I need to be here."

She nodded. "It's what makes you a good investigator, Julio. You really care about the animals. It's not about the prestige or anything like that. You want the animals to be safe."

His phone rang and he waved good-bye to her as he headed outside to answer it.

"Herendez."

"Hey, man, I got a guy here who'd really love to talk to you about some shit."

He grinned at the sound of Pedro's voice. "I think I know who you're talking about."

"*Hermano,* he's really upset and I think worried, though I don't think his concern is for his uncle. He's worried about the dogs."

"I'm not surprised." Julio checked his watch. "I have to get back to headquarters, but tell him I'll stop by around eight tonight. I'll tell him as much as I can."

"Thanks, bro. I'll see you tonight."

Julio shut his phone and strolled to his truck. After climbing in, he stared at the outdoor runs where some of the Caesar dogs paced or played. What could he tell BB about the dogs? Most of them were doing all right. Staying too long in a shelter wasn't the optimum thing for them either, but it was better than fighting for a living.

As he pulled out of the parking lot, Julio couldn't help but think BB and the dogs had been given a second chance, and he was going to do his best to make sure they were given every opportunity to make the best of it.

*   *   *

"I might have a witness from inside Caesar's operation who can tell us even more details." Julio met Captain Emerson's gaze with a rather bland expression. He didn't want to promise anything until he talked to BB.

"Why haven't you brought him in yet?" Emerson's jaw clenched like he was grinding his teeth.

"Because I haven't had time to talk to him, and I don't even know if he'll do it. I'm going to see him tonight and ask." Julio stuffed his hands in his jeans and rocked back on his heels. "I know I should've said something sooner, but he's a kid, barely out of his teens, and Caesar abused him just as much as he did the dogs."

"How do you know?"

"You saw the video from the last fight I went to, right?"

Emerson nodded.

"The blond kid in the video is Caesar's nephew. From what I could tell, he took care of the dogs, but Caesar sold him to customers for sex."

"God damn." Emerson slammed his fist on the table. "The more I hear about Caesar Addison, the more I hate the guy. So we could bring him up on prostitution charges, and it would be worse because the kid's underage."

Julio shrugged. "I don't think he's underage, Captain."

"Not now, but I guarantee he was when Caesar started selling him. That sort of thing usually kicks in as soon as the pimp realizes how much money he can get for underage whores." Emerson snarled in disgust. "See if he'll testify. We'll move him to a safe house and protect him."

"He's in a safe place right now. I don't want to move him unless we absolutely have to. I'll talk to him and see what he has to say, but I know one thing. He's going to want to see the dogs. He didn't fight them. I think he did everything he could to protect them. Of course, he was a kid, so what could he do but patch them up afterward?"

Emerson studied him for a moment before nodding. "Sounds good to me. What should we do about the dogs, though?"

Julio switched gears and settled into one of the chairs in the conference room. "I think we need to get evaluations on each animal like they did in that other case. Make a judgment on the individual dog, not the pack as a whole. It's not fair to them to be punished for something they couldn't stop. We have to be their voice, Captain. We can't let prevailing prejudices doom these dogs."

"That'll take money, which we don't have." Emerson sat across from him and rested his elbows on the table.

"There's been a fund started already for the care of the dogs. The more media we get on them, the more donations will pour in. I admit it'll only be a drop in the bucket compared to what we need to keep these animals, but it'll help. We need to let people know they aren't killing machines. That they're dogs, just like the family pet, but unlike their pets, these dogs were abused and didn't have a great start in life."

Emerson narrowed his eyes and glared at the papers in front of him. "That could work. I'll get our PR guys on it. I'll talk to the other animal protection groups. Maybe with this part of the case, at least, we can branch out and draw more people in."

"I know some people who would help, not only with the funding, but with the care of the dogs as well. There are also rescue groups out there willing to take them in and rehabilitate them. It'll take a while, though, which is why we need the money."

"The front office has already gotten calls from groups. We're just waiting on the case to go to trial. As soon as we can get the dogs awarded to the Humane Society by the court, we can figure out where they can go." Emerson gestured toward the door. "Why don't you go and talk to your potential witness? Try and convince him it'll help the dogs if he testifies. I'll get working on the rest."

"Yes, sir." Julio stood and went to the door, pausing before turning around. "Captain, can I take him to see the dogs?"

Emerson pursed his lips while he thought. "Sure. I don't see how that can hurt. None of them could be hurt by seeing someone they associate with good things."

"Thanks, sir."

Julio left, satisfied his boss would do everything he could to get the best possible outcome for the dogs. Looking at his watch, he found he had enough time to head home and shower before he went over to

Pedro's place.

* * *

BB stood in the living room of Pedro's house, hands clenched together to keep them from shaking. God, why was he so nervous? It wasn't like Juke was coming to drag him back to his uncle's. Hell, there wasn't anything left to go back to. The feds had taken everything and wouldn't let anyone onto the property. He'd tried to go there two days after the raid.

He frowned when he remembered the call he'd gotten from Aunt Daisy. She'd screamed at him for not being there when the agents came. Yet, he couldn't figure out what she thought he'd have been able to do if he'd been there. There wasn't any way he could have stopped them from finding everything.

He rubbed his chest over his pounding heart. Could he find the courage to tell Juke about it? He had a feeling Juke would want him to tell him everything he knew about Uncle Caesar's operation, and BB didn't know if he could. Shit, he didn't even want to talk to Pedro about what had happened to him, and Pedro had admitted he'd done the same thing until Juke got him out away from his former life.

Who the fuck was Juke? Or maybe his name was Julio. At least, that's what Pedro called him. How had he known about the agents raiding Caesar's place? Was he one of those undercover agents BB had seen on TV shows? That would explain how he'd known and why he chose to help BB with Queenie.

Queenie. How was she? He wanted to see her, but he didn't know where Juke had taken her.

A knock sounded on the door and he jumped. He admitted to himself, deep inside, he feared someone would come and take him back to his family, and he didn't want that at all. Pedro peered into the living room and gave BB a reassuring smile before heading to the front door.

"Hey, Julio, good to see you, man."

"It's been a crazy week, Pedro. I'll try to do better."

So Juke's real name *was* Julio. BB stared down at the floor. How did one greet the man who saved your life and the lives of those you held most dear? While he wasn't inclined to be touchy-feely, he had the urge to run and hug Julio. Why did he feel safer when the man was near? BB shook his head. It was all too confusing, and he didn't have the time to work it out in his head.

"BB's waiting for you in the living room. Can I get you something to drink?"

"A soda would be great."

Julio must be a regular visitor since he knew not to ask for a beer or alcohol. Pedro didn't allow it in the house, and BB wouldn't touch the stuff if his life depended on it. He'd seen what alcohol had done to his uncle and aunt, and he wasn't going down that road.

"Hey, BB, good to see you, man."

Looking up, he froze, stunned to see the handsome man standing in front of him. Why had he never noticed how hot Juke/Julio was? Most of the fights took place in the barn where the lighting wasn't the greatest and BB spent his time in the back with the dogs. He rarely mingled with the crowds because he didn't want anyone to spot him and ask his uncle about him. So he'd never paid attention to Julio when he was around.

Julio's shoulder-length black hair was caught at the nape of his neck with a leather thong, but it glistened under the lights like it was still damp from a shower. His tan skin attested to his Hispanic ancestry, as did his dark eyes. He towered over BB by a good six inches, making the man around six-four or five. Julio's black T-shirt drew tight over his chest and arms, showing off well-developed muscles. Faded blue jeans graced Julio's lower half, giving a tantalizing glimpse of the man's package.

BB jerked away his gaze. Shit, he shouldn't be thinking about any guy's cock, much less the man who thought of him as a kid.

"Hey, Juke." He paused. "Or should I say Julio?"

Julio smiled and something jumped under BB's skin. "Yeah. My name is Julio Herendez. I work for the Humane Society as one of their animal cruelty investigators. I was working undercover to bust your uncle's dog-fighting ring."

"Yeah, I kind of figured that out." BB folded his arms over his chest, not sure what to do.

Pedro returned with two glasses and a plate of cookies. "Here you go, Julio. I brought you a glass as well, BB. Also, I know how much you love Mama's cookies, so I brought some of those. She dropped them off the other night."

"How's your mama doing?" Julio took one of the glasses and the plate. He walked over to the couch and sat, setting the plate on the coffee table, along with a file folder.

"She's doing good, and she'll be happy to know you asked about her. I'll leave you two to talk. Come say good-bye before you leave, Julio."

"Will do, *hermano.*"

After Pedro left, silence settled over them while Julio ate three cookies in a row. BB sat in the chair to the left of the couch, watching the other man. Julio hummed happily.

"Pedro was right. You really do like his mother's cookies."

"Have you had one?" Julio winked and smiled.

"No. I don't do sugar very well. Tends to hype me up a lot, so Aunt Daisy cut me off when she figured it out. Having to deal with me took time away from her drinking."

He snapped his mouth shut. He didn't want to talk about his family. Julio nodded, like he understood what else BB was saying without having BB go into details.

"How's Queenie doing?" Changing the subject seemed the best idea since he didn't want to get into any more personal information.

Julio pushed the folder over in BB's direction. "She's doing really great. The vet says she'll need a little while longer before she's back to a hundred percent."

BB snatched the folder up and opened it, flipping through the pictures. The black-and-white pit bull female featured prominently in each photo. Often in each picture, there were two other dogs, both pits. The pure white looked like he was still a puppy, while the reddish brown one was older and had the scars of a fighting dog. Queenie looked happy with the other dogs, and BB smiled.

"She's pretty good with my dogs, so if she were to be adopted out, her new family shouldn't have a problem with other pets." Julio emptied his glass and leaned back against the cushions.

"Those are your dogs?" He held up a picture that had all three dogs in it.

"Yep. The white one is Samson, and the red one is Delilah. She runs our little pack, and Queenie seems fine with that."

"Both of them are pits?"

"I adopted them after my agency busted up a fighting ring. Delilah was one of the kennel's best fighters and it took me a year or two before she trusted me completely. Samson had never been fought, so all he needed was to be taught how to behave. He got that down after a couple months, though he's a work in progress."

Julio chuckled, and BB joined in, knowing what puppies were like.

"Is Queenie at a shelter?" He hoped not.

29

BB had been in shelters before when Caesar looked for bait dogs. He'd seen how dogs left in the shelter too long turned into mental cases. His dogs already had a disadvantage. He didn't want them to have to suffer anymore.

"No. She's living with me. I didn't want to turn her in, so I didn't say anything about her." Julio shrugged. "So I'm going against protocol here, but I think I can be forgiven this once."

BB stood and moved to sit next to Julio on the couch. He rested his hand on Julio's knee and squeezed.

"Thanks for taking care of her. I've took care of her since she was a pup. She's six now. I can't tell you how happy I am you took her, and you busted my uncle. I don't know how much longer I'd have lasted. It was driving me crazy, having to take care of the dogs, plus what Uncle Caesar wanted from me."

"It was only a matter of time, BB. Caesar was getting too big, trusting too much in certain people helping him. Well, those people can't help him. Actually, they can't help him because they're being busted as well." Julio turned to face him. "What does BB stand for?"

"You don't really want to know, and it ain't got anything to do with my name." His cheeks burned at the thought of telling Julio what his nickname really meant.

"What's your name then?"

"Paine," BB mumbled.

Julio leaned a little closer. "Your mother named you Paine?"

"Actually, my aunt. Mom split the day they let her outta the hospital. She dropped me at Aunt Daisy's and took off with her dealer. Aunt Daisy said I would cause her nothing but pain the rest of my life. That's what they called me."

"Jesus, that sucks, man. Hope you don't mind me saying your family is fucked up."

BB stared down at the table. "You don't have to tell me that. I figured from early on I didn't have much chance to make to my twentieth birthday. I'm two years beyond it, but I figured my luck was ending soon."

"Can I call you Paine? Or is there something else you'd like me to call you?" Julio didn't seem inclined to call him BB anymore.

"Paine is fine. I'm not attached to it or anything. Been called BB for so long, probably won't answer to Paine right away."

"Maybe someday you'll tell me what BB means."

"Not likely," he muttered.

Julio nodded and tensed slightly. "I have something to ask you, Paine, and I don't want your answer right away. You need to think about what I'm going to ask you. Oh, and I got permission to take you to the shelter to see the dogs. I think they're missing you."

"Have you seen them?" Excitement rushed through him at the thought of seeing the animals he'd grown to love.

"Yes, I go to visit them every chance I get. I don't always get to stay long, but at least I take one or two of them out for a walk or play with the ones who do play." Julio chuckled. "I think I've fallen in love with Stu. That big guy reminds me of Delilah, tough when he needs to be, but God, once he trusts you, he'll kill himself for you."

BB sighed. "That's what made him a grand champion. Didn't matter how hurt he was, he'd do whatever Uncle Caesar wanted. I'd spend days getting him healed up, then my uncle would take him to another fight. It was only a matter of time before he got too hurt for me to doctor him up."

Julio shifted, and BB realized he'd been leaning on the man. He shot to his feet and paced, putting the coffee table between them. *What an idiot.* Except for the touch to his face the night he last saw him, BB had never gotten the feeling Julio liked guys. Maybe BB shouldn't be attracted to guys, but even after all the guys who'd fucked him without his permission, he still found men attractive.

Nothing said needy or desperate than clinging to the first person to show him kindness. He gave himself a mental shake and focused on what else Julio had said.

"What did you need to ask me?"

Julio straightened his shoulders, seeming to brace himself. "First of all, I want to reiterate that you seeing the dogs isn't contingent on you agreeing to do what I want."

"I don't understand."

"Remember the last night I saw you?"

BB nodded as his stomach roiled. God, he felt like a pile of shit. How could Julio ever respect him after seeing him like that?

"Caesar told you to do what he wanted, or the puppy would suffer. You went with the bastard because you didn't want the pup to get hurt."

"He's just a baby. He don't deserve to be treated like shit, especially when I can prevent it. It's not like I was gonna die or anything. Letting someone fuck me don't mean nothing."

Christ, he fought the need to rub his chest again as he spouted those lies. It meant everything the first time his uncle had sold him to some creepy old man. It broke something in him. Maybe that was why he didn't think Julio would consider him as anything other than the poor kid whose uncle pimped him out. He didn't deserve anything more than pity or contempt. Hell, he'd allowed it to happen.

Julio clenched his fists and tension crept into BB's body. It was like the man wanted to reach out and shake BB, but didn't want to risk touching him. Of course, touching a used whore like BB probably grossed Julio out.

"That's sort of what I'm saying. I'm not giving you a 'do this or else' option. If you choose not to do what I ask, it doesn't matter. I'll still take you to see the dogs."

"Okay."

Julio breathed deeply and bent forward, bracing his elbows on his knees and letting his clasped hands dangle between his legs. "I talked to my captain and told him I might have a witness from inside the organization who might consider turning federal witness on this case."

BB stayed silent, working out what Julio said. Ratting out his uncle? Did he have the courage to do that? He didn't have a problem telling Julio about the dogs, but did Julio want information about the other stuff? Uncle didn't just sell BB's ass. He sold his daughters to men, plus he sold meth. BB was sure the feds hadn't found Uncle Caesar's lab. His uncle didn't keep that near the kennels, knowing things could go wrong. Caesar wasn't willing to risk both of his businesses.

"What do you want me to talk about?"

"Everything."

He turned away from Julio, dropping his chin to his chest and closing his eyes. "I don't think I can. Some things aren't for others to hear."

BB jumped when two hands landed on his shoulders. The warmth leaking from Julio's body soaked into BB's back and he resisted the need to lean back on the bigger man.

"I understand it'd be hard for you to talk about what happened to you, Paine, but the more we know about Caesar's operation, the more felonies we can charge him with. He'll be going to jail for a long time, and he can't hurt you or the dogs anymore."

Snorting, BB hitched his shoulders slightly, not wanting to knock Julio's hands off. He didn't like people touching him usually, but there was something different about Julio.

"It'll be embarrassing and upsetting, but don't you want your uncle to get what's coming to him? I wish the sentences for dog-fighting were stiffer, but they aren't. If we don't get the evidence to charge Caesar with other crimes, he'll be out in two years, and I'm afraid you'll be right back where you were."

"I don't know if I can sit up in front of people and talk about what guys did to me. It's pathetic, ya know, that I didn't do nothing to stop them." He bit his lip, forcing his tears back.

Julio swung him around and lifted his chin with his finger until their gazes met. "Tell me, Paine, what *could* you have done? You were a child, I'm sure, the first time it happened. How were you supposed to stop it, especially when your aunt wasn't any help either? Am I right?"

"She does nothing but drink all day. Never said nothing, not even when Uncle Caesar sold little Katie to some bastard. He got a hundred bucks for one night for her. She ain't never been the same. I try to help her, but she don't trust people no more. And Uncle kept selling her and Betsy. He beat me bloody a couple times when I stood up to him about that. It's one thing to sell me. I can take it. Just sex. Don't mean nothing, but they're just children."

"Who are Betsy and Katie?"

BB mentally slapped himself. He hadn't meant to mention the girls. He'd planned on going to his uncle's tomorrow and seeing if the girls were still there. There hadn't been any mention of them in the news reports.

"My cousins—Uncle Caesar's daughters. Katie's sixteen and Betsy's fourteen."

"Fucking bastard. If he wasn't in prison, I'd hunt him down and rip him apart."

The anger in Julio's voice eased BB in some strange way. BB reached up and patted one of Julio's hands.

"It's all right. I'm not worth getting yourself in trouble for."

"No one deserves to be treated like a possession. You're a person, Paine. You deserve as much respect as anyone else in the world. Your uncle never should've done what he did to you or your cousins."

"Or the dogs," he added, trying to ignore how Julio's hot breath bathing his cheek turned him on.

"Yeah, the dogs, too. I'll be beside you the entire way, Paine. I won't let anything happen to you, and no one's going to treat you badly either."

"Would you make Katie or Betsy testify about what Uncle Caesar did to them? They can't deal with all this shit, Julio. They ain't strong like me. They're fragile." BB closed his eyes as he told the lie.

Fuck, he wasn't strong at all. Every minute Julio stood close to him, a piece of the wall around BB's heart crumbled. He didn't want Julio seeing him as weak. If he was going to do this, he had to act tough.

"No. I'll keep their names out of it. If I didn't want to make your uncle pay for as much as I can, I wouldn't even ask you to tell."

BB nodded. "Okay, I'll tell you all you want to know. First of all, you should call your federal agent friends and tell them there's a meth lab about five miles away from Uncle Caesar's place. He's been dealing meth for the past six years."

Surprise widened Julio's eyes. "No fucking way?"

"Yeah. Meth ain't that hard to make, you know. Do it all in one pot nowadays."

"Holy shit." Julio stepped away from him and fumbled in his pocket to pull out a phone. "I have to call my captain. Can you give me directions to Caesar's meth lab? I want to get the DEA and law enforcement out there before someone figures out you're talking." Julio pulled out a paper of paper and pushed it toward BB.

"I don't know how to write nothing except my name really, and can't read very well either." Shame caused BB to drop his head.

"Okay. Tell me and I'll write it down, so Emerson can let the proper authorities know."

BB did and before Julio could call his captain, BB told him, "Tell them to be careful. The guys at the lab have shotguns, and Uncle told them to use them if necessary. Most of the guys are addicts, so they're paranoid. Also, there are a couple of dogs on the property, usually tied up to two abandoned trucks at the edge of the road. Try not to kill those dogs. They ain't done nothing wrong to no one and they're friendly. Mostly they're just there to bark and alert the others."

Julio nodded. "I'll tell them to tranq the dogs and take them to the shelter where the other dogs are. I'm sure they can take two more, and you can see them when you visit."

"I'll get some more cookies and drinks."

BB grabbed the plate and glasses before heading to the kitchen. It was going to be a long night, but BB kept the knowledge he would get to see the dogs first and foremost in his mind. That would be his reward for bearing his scars to Julio.

CHAPTER 4

Julio tapped his pencil on the notepad, rereading what he'd written about the night he witnessed Caesar sell BB. Paine, Julio corrected his thoughts. He didn't think he wanted to know what BB stood for after seeing the way Paine reacted to it.

"When's your witness getting here, Herendez?" Emerson poked his head around the doorframe to glare at him.

After checking his watch, Julio looked over at his boss. "He'll be here in a few minutes. You have to cut him some slack, Captain. This isn't going to be easy for him. As soon as we're done for the day, taking down his statement, I'm going to run him over to the shelter to see the dogs. He's going to need something encouraging after this."

"Fine with me. As long as he doesn't run out on us, I don't care what you do with him." His boss waved a hand at him before disappearing again.

"I highly doubt that," Julio muttered under his breath.

If his boss knew exactly what Julio wanted to do with Paine, Emerson would probably pitch a fit. Not that Emerson was a homophobe or anything, but because Paine was a witness, Julio needed to keep his hands off him. Thank God his boss and most of the agents he worked with were rather open-minded about his orientation. He didn't flaunt it or anything like that, but he also didn't try to keep who he dated a secret.

Paine was so beautiful and broken that Julio just wanted to wrap his arms around the younger man and hold him close. He wanted to tell

Paine he wouldn't allow anyone to hurt him again, but Paine wouldn't believe him. Not when so many who should have protected him had let him down. And really, did he think Paine would just trust him when he didn't even know Julio?

Did he want a relationship with the younger man? Or try to have a relationship with him? Julio didn't have time to date, and his personality wasn't the type to enjoy one-night stands. Would Paine be open to trying to date or was he too damaged from the abuse he suffered all those years?

"Hey, Herendez, that guy you were waiting for is here." One of the other agents leaned around the door and informed him.

"Thanks. Is the front desk sending him up or do I have to go down and get him?"

"Nah. They're sending him up."

Julio checked to make sure he had the recorder. He'd type the transcript up for Paine to sign after the entire interview was done. He planned to take the younger man to the shelter later on that day. He was going to let Paine go at his own pace during the telling. It did need to be done as soon as possible, but Julio didn't want the whole situation to freak Paine out.

Someone cleared his throat, and Julio looked up to see Paine standing in the doorway. He stood up and held out his hand to the young blond.

"Good to see you, Paine. I'm glad you agreed to do this here at headquarters."

Paine ducked his head and peeked through his long bangs at Julio. His plump lips smiled, and Julio's cock stiffened. Christ, he couldn't go through this whole interview with a hard-on. He had to try to be professional about this. When Paine's hand slipped into his, Julio gritted his teeth to keep from groaning.

"Anything I can do to send my uncle away for as long as possible." Paine jerked his hand up and down once before dropping it.

Julio stepped back, not wanting to crowd the man. "I thought we'd get started and go straight through until about three. Then I'll drive you over to the shelter, so you can see the dogs. I figured you'd need some loving from them after our conversation."

"Thanks. Can I see Queenie sometime soon?"

"Sure. If you want, we can go to my house before I take you back to Pedro's."

"Great." Paine nodded before wiping his hands on his pants and sitting down.

"Is your witness here yet?" Emerson burst into the room.

Paine jumped to his feet, worry shining in his eyes. Julio patted Paine's shoulder.

"He's right here, Captain. Paine Addison, this is my boss, Captain Emerson. He's the one heading the case against your uncle."

Emerson and Paine shook hands.

"We appreciate your willingness to do this, Mr. Addison. I understand how difficult this might be for you, but ultimately, it'll help the entire case. Herendez here will be your liaison officer. If you need or want anything, talk to him and he'll do his damnedest to get it for you."

"Yes, sir." Paine ducked his head again, not meeting Emerson's gaze.

Emerson shot Julio a narrow-eyed glare, and Julio shrugged.

"Well, I have to get back to all the paperwork this case is generating for me. Have a good day, Mr. Addison."

After Emerson left, Julio gestured for Paine to sit again. "Would you like something to drink? I can have someone bring us whatever you want."

"I'd just like some water." Paine clasped his hands on top of the table and licked his lips.

Julio went to the pitcher of water on a table sitting by one of the walls. He poured two glasses and brought them back to Paine.

"Here."

"Thanks." Paine took it, and Julio noticed how the man's hand shook slightly.

Sitting next to Paine, he rested his hand on the younger man's shoulder and squeezed. "I know this is hard, but trust me, no one's going to hassle you about this. Well, your uncle's defense attorney might, but we'll help you when/if it comes to that. Right now, it's just you and me. No one else will be in the room with us."

"Shouldn't there be someone else? I thought you needed someone else to listen to me talk."

"I didn't think you'd be comfortable with a stranger in the room."

Paine looked at him. "Ain't you a stranger? I mean, I don't know nothing about you really."

The guy had a point. Julio scrubbed a hand over his face. "All right. I'll bring someone else in as a witness along with me. If at any point, you feel uncomfortable or just want to be done for the day, tell me and we can start up again tomorrow."

Paine turned back to face the table, not saying anything else. Julio stood and went out to grab one of the other agents who worked on the case. He picked Maryanne, an older female agent. She gave off a strong maternal vibe, and Paine would probably react well to her presence.

She came in, and Julio introduced them. Paine stayed quiet, just shaking her hand and nodding. The longer they took to get started, the more nervous Paine was going to be. Julio understood that, so he quickly set everything up and sat across the table from Paine.

"Okay, Paine, I want you to start at the beginning."

Paine looked confused. "Beginning of what? The dog-fighting? The meth selling? The whoring his family out?"

Maryanne blinked in surprise, and Julio sighed.

"We'll be getting to those all in good time. Tell us how you came to be living with your uncle and his family."

Paine fidgeted with his glass, and Julio waited, letting Paine get to the start of his story in his own time. The young man took a deep breath, causing Julio to push the record button on the machine.

"My mom was a druggie whore, if you believe my uncle. I think she probably was, but hell, you know, she was my mom." Pausing, Paine took a sip before continuing. "She dumped me at Uncle Caesar's when I was about two days old. I didn't have a name or nothing. Aunt Daisy called me Paine 'cause she said I wouldn't bring nothing to the family but pain."

Julio grimaced, and Maryanne caught his gaze with her own pained expression. He nodded because he knew how she felt.

"I'm the oldest kid, I guess you could say. Katie was born six years after my uncle and aunt took me in. Then Betsy came along two years after that. I take care of them best I can because Aunt Daisy ain't capable of doing it herself. She drinks from the moment she gets up in the morning until she passes out at night. I guess I should be happy she ain't doing meth, right?"

Meeting Paine's eyes, Julio could see Paine wanted Julio's understanding about it. Clenching his hands, Julio simply nodded. He couldn't do what he really wanted, which was to go around the table and pull Paine into his arms. He wanted to whisper and reassure Paine that everything would be fine. Yet how could he be sure Paine's life would change, just because he was out of his uncle's world? He didn't know what kind of skills Paine had or at least what kind of marketable skills the man had.

Julio didn't want Paine ending up on the streets, selling himself to survive. Pedro had been kind enough to allow Paine a room in his house, but Pedro's partner, Santo, was returning from three months overseas. Julio needed to find somewhere else for Paine to live.

"Okay, so when I was ten, I guess, or maybe eleven, Uncle Caesar starts his kennel. He buys the dogs and puts me in charge of feeding them. So I do, and I take care of them like I'm doing with the girls. It gets to be too much, you know, so I stop going to school. The dogs need me. Little Katie and Betsy need me. Uncle Caesar and Aunt Daisy don't care whether I get book learning or not. They figure I'll stay around and help out with everything."

Paine hit his fist on the table and growled softly. Tears dripped onto the backs of his hands. Both Julio and Maryanne ignored them for the moment. The tension in Paine's shoulders told them he wouldn't welcome their touch.

"I don't want to live there no more. I want to see the world and what else is going on out there. I don't have no friends because I can't let them know what my uncle's doing. I'm ashamed of what I've done and what he does."

"Paine, you haven't done anything. Everything that's happened to you is your uncle's fault. I know this is hard for you to work through, but none of it is your fault. All you've done is try to keep things together for you and your cousins."

"I couldn't save them. He sold them, and I couldn't stop it from happening. When they came back, they were broken. All I could do was hold them. Aunt Daisy didn't say shit to them. She treated them like they were dirt under her feet. How can she do that when they're her children? I can understand why she didn't say nothing when he did it to me. I'm nothing to her, but to not stop him with her own children? That's what I don't understand."

Tears streamed down Paine's cheeks, and Julio got the feeling he cried for himself just as much as he shed those tears for his cousins.

"Do you remember who the men were Caesar sold the girls to? If you can remember, maybe we can charge them."

Paine wiped his face on his sleeve and chuckled harshly. "You probably got pictures of them at the fights. I'm sure you took pictures while you were wandering around the crowds."

"I could get you a viewing of the tapes and you can point out all the men your uncle sold you and your cousins to, okay?" Julio let his need take over for a second and he reached out, laying his hand over one of

Paine's. "Would you be able to do that?"

They stared at each other for a second, and Paine turned his hand over, entwining their fingers. The need in that touch cracked Julio's heart even more. There was so much strength in Paine.

"Paine, you amaze me. How you've managed to stay sane with everything that has happened to you is beyond me. God, I don't think you realize just how strong you are."

*   *   *

BB glanced down at Julio's hand clasped in his and tried to believe what Julio said. He just didn't see it. All he thought about was how many other men had used him. How they touched him to take something from him. Yet Julio's touch didn't grasp at him. The agent's hand seemed to support him and urge him to look beyond the prison of his uncle's making.

Shit, BB wanted to get free of those bars. He wanted to look beyond the narrow world he'd lived in. Maybe talking about it and spilling the dark secrets residing in his life would help him. He shook his head. He wasn't much for self-analyzing. All he wanted was the guilt and disgust to go away.

"How old were you when Caesar sold you the first time?"

Maryanne's voice surprised him. He'd forgotten the woman was in the room with them. Julio squeezed his hand once more before sitting back in his chair. BB tried not to think about how bereft he felt without Julio's touch.

Closing his eyes for a second, he took another deep breath, calming his pulse. His stomach roiled and all he really wanted was to find the nearest bathroom and throw up. Good thing he hadn't eaten anything before he came.

"Around my twelfth birthday. Uncle Caesar started me going to the fights with him around that same time. He couldn't handle the dogs well, but they listened to me. I hated it. First time I saw a fight, I puked my guts out until I had snot running down my face. How can people be like that?"

Maryanne shifted, but it was Julio who answered him.

"I wish I could give you an answer, Paine, but unfortunately some people don't see animals as having feelings or as important as humans. They don't understand we're all connected in some way. It's been pretty obvious that those who abuse animals will abuse people weaker

40

than themselves."

BB nodded and he knew his uncle was a good example of what Julio spoke about. The man wasn't happy unless he was hurting someone or something.

"Have you seen that man since?"

"Naw…he ended up dead about three years ago. Too much meth."

"Okay. How many people have you had to go with? And how often do you and the girls have to service Addison's business associates?"

"The first time Uncle Caesar owed this guy money, so he said he'd take me for the night instead. After that, Uncle figured he could get money for me. Started selling me to other people. Weren't always guys who paid for me. Some ladies did, too. Mostly after fights, though he sent me to some of the meth dealers as well."

BB didn't know what to say next. He drank the rest of his water and stood to get some more. When he turned, he caught Julio staring at him. BB recognized the lust in Julio's gaze. He'd seen it in other men's eyes as they watched him. Yet Julio's desire was tempered by an odd gentleness, something BB had never seen in the people he'd been involved with. He had seen it in others when they looked at someone they cared about.

Dropping his gaze, BB sifted through the confusion clouding his mind. Why would Julio care about him? He was an ignorant, used hick who didn't understand the world around him. His comfort zone was the dogs and he wanted to see them.

"Come and sit down, Paine. We'll talk a little more before calling it a day, and I take you out to the shelter." Julio stopped for a moment and seemed to be thinking.

"What?"

"I got an idea about a way you could earn some money while this case is going on. I'm not going to say anything until I talk to some people, but I think it'll be good for you."

"I'm not smart, Julio. I never finished high school. Hell, barely got through seventh grade before I quit." He hated admitting that.

"Don't worry. You're qualified for this job."

Well, Julio hadn't steered him wrong yet, so he'd trust the guy a little longer.

They sat for another hour. BB focused his recounting on the drugs and the dealers his uncle supplied. There were times BB had to make deliveries and his nerves would be shot by the time he got back to his uncle's place. He wasn't cut out to be a dealer.

He gave as detailed accounts as he could of different deals his uncle did and which suppliers Caesar worked with. As best he could, he came up with dates and amounts. Each question Julio asked in such a way BB realized he did know the answer. Uncle Caesar had thought he'd kept BB out of the business enough to be safe from BB ever rolling over on him, yet BB was smarter than anyone gave him credit for. Even BB hadn't realized how much he knew.

After an hour, Julio stood and stretched. BB averted his gaze, not wanting either Julio or Maryanne to catch him ogling Julio. Wouldn't do to have his interest known. He was a witness to a huge case. Julio was smart and wasn't about to mess up his chance to nail Uncle Caesar to the wall by messing around with one of his star witnesses. BB's mind understood that, but his body and his heart wished Julio would bend the rules just a little. Maybe enough to kiss him.

BB wanted to know what it was like to kiss a guy because *he* wanted to, not because the asshole had paid his uncle for the opportunity. Everything in BB cried out to be held because of who he was inside, not because of how pretty his outsides were.

"Paine, you ready to go?"

Standing, he nodded. "Yeah. I guess."

"Okay. I'll have one of the secretaries type this up and you can sign it tomorrow when you come back for our second session."

BB shrugged, not really interested one way or the other about the report. His mind focused on the dogs and getting to see them. He'd missed all of them. It was hard not having them to take care of anymore. Watching TV at Pedro's house had been nice for a day or two, but he'd gotten bored while Pedro was at work.

He followed Julio through the outer area filled with desks and people. Some worked on computers, while others talked on the phone. A few were grouped around one desk, discussing something. He wasn't close enough to figure out what they were talking about. Julio stopped outside an office and knocked on the door.

"Come in."

Julio stuck his head around the opened door. "Hey, Captain, I'm heading out to take Paine Addison to see the Caesar dogs."

"Good. How'd it go?"

"Really good. We got information on Addison's meth lab. I know Maryanne gave you those papers."

"Yeah. Waiting to hear on the warrant as we speak. The DEA and FBI are ready to go in whenever we get it."

Julio braced a shoulder against the doorframe. "We also might want to consider taking Addison's daughters from his wife and putting them in foster care. We have to figure out where they are first. Nothing's been seen of Daisy Addison since Caesar was taken into custody."

"What? Wait," BB protested. "Do you mean the girls might have been left alone?"

Looking over his shoulder at him, Julio frowned. "They shouldn't stay in that situation any longer. With your uncle in jail and your aunt drunk most of the time, I'm not sure it's the best thing for them to be left on their own. We don't know. After the agents went through Caesar's house, no one's been back there since. It's safer for them to be out of there, even if your aunt was still there."

"I can take care of them. Been doing it most of my life." BB hesitated. "I just don't got a place for us all to stay."

"That's something else I need to talk to you about, Captain. The place where I have Paine isn't going to be available much longer. I was wondering if I could put him in one of our safe houses. Maybe if his cousins agree to leave, they could stay with him there."

"That's fine, but you're on protection detail for him. I can only spare you and one other agent, Herendez."

"Thanks, sir."

Julio stepped back and shut the door behind him. BB grabbed his arm and pulled him to a stop. "Why can't I stay at Pedro's?"

"Because Pedro's partner, Santo, is returning tomorrow. He's been overseas for three months doing contract work in Iraq. He's not going to be in the best of moods, so it's best if you're out of there."

BB stiffened. "He won't hurt Pedro, will he?"

Julio laughed. "More than likely, it'll be Pedro hitting Santo when the man irritates him too much. It's nothing like that. Santo'll be tense and grumpy for a while until he finally adjusts to being back here. It'll be easier for everyone if you don't have to deal with that."

"Okay, as long as he don't hurt Pedro. He's been a decent guy to me, opening his house like that to someone he don't even know." BB liked Pedro, even though he seemed a little weird at times.

"Yeah, well, their relationship is a little strange, but it works for them, so who am I to judge?" Julio clapped BB on the shoulder. "Let's go grab something to eat on the way to the shelter."

BB's stomach growled at that moment, and Julio smiled.

"Sounds good. Were you serious about taking the girls from my aunt?"

Julio nodded toward another agent as they walked from the room. "Yeah. Your cousins need help, Paine, and they aren't going to get it from your aunt. Medical and mental help probably. It's rough having your own father treat you like you were nothing more than a dog."

BB snorted. "He treated his dogs better."

"And see, that's not right. A true man treats everyone and every creature with respect. He doesn't beat them, make them fight, or allow others to treat them like shit."

Anger deepened Julio's voice, and BB shivered at the thought of what pleasure could do to that voice.

"Well, if you think they should leave, I'll go with you to get them. They're broken, but they trust me. Ain't never hurt them and took a couple beatings instead of them." BB still wasn't confident Julio's idea was the best, but he'd go along with it as long as the girls didn't pitch a fit.

"Thanks, Paine."

Julio gestured to a plain brown four-door sedan and unlocked it for him. BB settled into the seat, hungry and anxious. The first day of telling his story hadn't gone as bad as he thought it would. Maybe he could get through the rest without losing what was left of his self respect.

CHAPTER 5

"Here we are."

BB sat up and looked out the window of Julio's car. He'd been dozing since finishing his burger and fries. They rolled to a stop in front of rather non-descript building. The only thing marking it as a shelter was the fenced-in yard in back that BB could see just the edge of.

He jumped out of the car and headed around the side. There were several large dog runs extending from the building. A single dog stood in each one. As soon as he appeared, the dogs started barking. He heard the joy in those barks. None of them sounded angry or aggressive.

"Hey there, Louisa."

BB knelt down in front of the first kennel, where a red brindle pit bull female stood, her tail whipping back and forth. She licked his fingers and whined as he petted her wide, square head.

"How've you been, girl?"

He looked her over and liked what he saw. Louisa had been one of the dogs who'd fought the night before the raid. She'd been pretty tore up, but her wounds looked like they were healing nicely.

"The vet stitched her up. She'll always have scars, but at least she didn't have any serious wounds." Julio stopped a few feet away from him, but didn't try to approach any closer.

BB studied Louisa and noticed that, while she kept an eye on Julio, she didn't tense or curl her lip in warning. Not surprising since Louisa had always been one of the better-adjusted dogs, even with being fought several times.

"Thanks. I was worried about her. Can I go in with her? How much time do I have?"

Julio checked his watch and reached out slowly to ruffle BB's hair. "Take as long as you'd like. I don't have anywhere to be except an empty house. I have a fenced-in back yard and the dogs can let themselves out into it. I left them enough water to keep them happy for a while and I fed them before I came to meet up with you. We're good."

"Great."

"Julio, who'd you bring with you?" An older gentleman walked around the building and greeted Julio.

BB stood when Julio gestured to him.

"This is Paine Addison."

The man's friendly smile froze and coldness seeped into his eyes. BB eased back, knowing what a look like that usually meant.

"Yes, he's Caesar Addison's nephew, but he had nothing to do with fighting the dogs. He took care of them the best he could without getting himself killed. I wouldn't be surprised if he's the reason why most of these dogs are as socialized as they are." Julio stepped in front of BB, almost like he was trying to protect him. "Watch how the dogs react to him."

Julio gestured behind them, and BB turned to see Louisa pressed against the cage door, trying her damnedest to get as close to BB as possible.

"Xavier, I'll stay with him the entire time, but I think it'll do the dogs good to have Paine visit them. I want him to play with them, take them out for walks, do whatever he used to do with them while they were at Caesar's. He never fought them or trained them to fight."

"I'm not sure." Xavier hesitated.

"Come on." Julio held up his hands. "Paine knows these dogs better than anyone else. He knows which ones don't like other dogs or which ones might be a threat to people. Why not take advantage of his expertise? I think you should give him a job here at the shelter to help with them. They're going to be here for a while. We still haven't gotten a judge to sign them over to the Humane Society. Until that happens, you're not going to be able to take in any other dogs."

Louisa whined, and BB crouched, slipping his fingers through the gaps in the wire to stroke over her muzzle. He could feel Xavier's gaze boring between his shoulder blades, but he refused to look at the man.

It pissed him off that he would be tarred with the same brush as his uncle. He had a temper, but he never took his anger out on defenseless creatures, human or otherwise. Hell, he rarely resorted to violence, mostly just yelling and pacing.

He'd learned a long time ago, violence solved nothing. All it did was breed resentment and more violence. There had been dogs that'd been fought too much, or over-bred until they lost their minds. Those were the ones who turned on him. He'd been bitten many times, but never punished them because it wasn't their fault. He placed the blame solely where it needed to be—on his uncle. The bastard deserved to rot in prison for what he did to the dogs and his own daughters.

"Fine, Julio, but you're responsible for him. I'll keep an eye on him and we'll talk later."

Julio's hand landed on BB's head, trailing his fingers through BB's curls. BB froze, not wanting Julio to realize what he was doing and stop.

"Just give him a chance. That's all I'm asking. Hell, that's all I'm asking for all the dogs as well. They just need a chance to show how much love they have to give to the right person."

Did Julio mean BB as well as the dogs? Did he think BB still had the ability to love? Would Julio accept BB's love if he ever got up the courage to say something? BB snorted to himself. What did he know about love? And why was he thinking about that emotion in connection with Julio?

Ignoring the man behind him, BB rested his forehead against the fence, and Louisa licked him with a short swipe of her tongue. He laughed and wiped off his face.

"Here. If she's one you can trust out on a leash, why don't you take her for a walk? She gets to run in the kennel, but still it's nice to go out and sniff around."

He took the leash and unhooked the cage door. Gesturing for Louisa to sit, he waited until she kept sitting for a minute before he clipped the leash to her collar. Julio stepped back as BB brought Louisa out. BB glanced up and smiled at Julio.

"Is there a dog in the pack that Louisa likes? Maybe I could grab him/her and walk with you. It's better to have another person to walk with."

"Reggie. He's a little black-and-tan pup. Got a chewed up ear." He grimaced. "One of the other kennel's dogs got out and attacked him. Reggie fought like a champ, but the other dog outweighed him by at least thirty pounds. I had to beat the stupid thing off the pup."

Julio's lip curled in disgust. "What'd your uncle do?"

"He wanted to kill Reggie. Said that getting chewed on like he did made him a piss-poor fighter. I wouldn't let him do it. Took a beating for it, but ended up nursing Reggie back to health. He hadn't been truly fought yet. Uncle was training him, though."

"But he'll be okay with Louisa?"

BB nodded. "Yeah, they like each other."

"Okay." Julio grabbed another leash off the table next to the entryway. "Let's go find Reggie."

As they wandered around the shelter looking for Reggie, BB glanced in each cage, checking out the dog inside. Big Stu barked at him, but it was Julio the pit looked at.

"I think Stu likes you." BB tilted his head in the black dog's direction.

Julio smiled and went over to scratch Stu's head. "That's because I like Stu. He's a pretty awesome dog. Is he good with other dogs?"

"For the most part. At least female dogs. He's not big on males—dogs or otherwise, except me and you obviously."

"Hmmm…I wonder about that. I have Samson and Delilah. Oh, and Queenie. I was kind of hoping Stu would be okay with Samson."

"Why?" BB heard an excited yip, and Louisa dragged him over to where Reggie was practically climbing the door of his cage. "Here's Reggie."

Julio joined him and soon they were briskly walking down one of the trails near the shelter. The dogs sniffed their way around, going in one direction, then the other. They did their damnedest to tangle up the leashes.

"Why do you want Samson to get along with Stu?"

"What?" Julio blinked, chasing away whatever thoughts were running around his brain. "Oh, I'd like to adopt him when they're released from the shelter. I think he'd fit in well with my group."

BB thought about it. He'd never actually seen Stu go after another dog unless they were in the ring. Mostly Stu just ignored them.

"Maybe if you introduced them in a neutral environment. That way neither dog is defending his turf."

Julio chuckled. "His turf? I told you Delilah runs my pack. I think if Stu tried anything with Samson, Delilah would take him down a peg or two. Would you be willing to help me out? Stu knows you and trusts you. He might react better to another dog if you were around."

"Sure." He'd agree to anything that would give him more time with the dogs and Julio.

They spent several hours with the animals, taking each out of their cages and playing with them or walking two dogs at a time. The ones who seemed a little more skittish got extra attention. All the dogs went out of their mind with joy whenever BB approached them.

BB sat on the ground under one of the large oak trees with Pippi, a white pit bull female. He loved her because she had a black spot at the tip of her tail, but that was the only color she had. She was like a little smooth blanket of snow as she sprawled out beside him, chewing on her Kong toy.

Julio had gotten a phone call, so he stood a few feet away, discussing something with whomever had called him. Footsteps approached BB and he glanced up to see Xavier heading toward him. He couldn't help but tense, and Pippi sensed his unease. She lifted her head and whined at him. He ran his hand down her back and shushed her.

"Julio knows me too well."

BB stayed silent, and Xavier stopped near him, crossed his arms over his chest, and stared down at him.

"I saw how the dogs act around you, and I'll admit you have a way with them. If you'd ever hurt them, they wouldn't have accepted your touch as readily as they do. I can tell they love you." Xavier sighed. "Would you like to help out here? I have volunteers, but most of them are leery around the pits and it causes behavioral problems with the dogs. I could even pay you a small salary. There's a fund set up for the care of the Caesar dogs. I can tap into that."

A salary? Being paid to do something he liked doing was a novel concept for BB. Yet he liked the idea of it. He bit his lip and shot a glance over at Julio. Would it be all right for him to work with the dogs? Would his presence at the shelter cause problems with the case?

Julio snapped his phone shut and slipped it into his pocket. BB dropped his gaze, his need for the man swelling in him. Christ, he didn't want Julio to see how much he desired him. No man in his right man would want a guy whored out by his uncle. And he didn't even know for sure Julio was gay. Julio seemed accepting of Pedro and Santo's relationship, but that didn't mean anything. He could just be a very open-minded friend.

"What's up, Paine?"

"Xavier said I could work at the shelter with the dogs. He'd even pay me a little for it. Says there's a fund or something."

"I don't think there'll be too much of a problem."

Xavier glared at Julio. "You set me up, didn't you? You knew as soon as I saw how Paine was with the dogs, I'd be asking him to work here."

"I was hoping." Julio checked his watch. "Hey, Paine, we have to head out. I was supposed to take you to a safe house, but it's not ready. You can stay with me tonight, so we'll stop by Pedro's to get your stuff."

"I don't have much. Just one change of clothes. That's all, but I'd like to pick up my truck." BB stood, brushed off his jeans, and took Pippi back to her cage.

"That's a good idea. Make it easier for you to get back here to the shelter tomorrow. I should get home. My dogs are pretty self-sufficient for the most part as long as I don't ignore them for too long."

"Good. I'll see you tomorrow then. You can come whenever you want. Julio has a key." Xavier held out his hand. "I'll have papers ready for you to sign as well."

BB shook Xavier's hand, his heart in his throat. He'd never held a real job before. Hopefully, there wouldn't be any reason why he couldn't work with the dogs. This way he could pay Pedro back for letting him crash at his house the past week. "I'll do my best, sir."

"Hell, anyone watching you can see how much you love these dogs. It's a bad hand you've all been dealt, but I think, with a little help, you'll all make it."

BB wasn't entirely sure about that, but he thanked Xavier for the sentiment. He climbed in the car with Julio, trying hard not to think about spending the night under the same roof as the other man.

*   *   *

Julio grinned as Queenie knocked Paine over in her exuberance at seeing him again. His two dogs skirted around the pile and greeted him with licks and tail wags. He crouched, giving out pats and scratches, while keeping an eye on Paine and Queenie. After his dogs lost interest in him and moved on to sniffing Paine, Julio stood and stretched, groaning as his back popped. Paine looked at him from where he lay on the floor, surrounded by dogs.

"Getting old. I'm going to grab a shower and change. While you're cleaning up, I'll get dinner started."

Paine scrambled to his feet. "I can help with dinner."

"Good. I'll have you make the salad. I'm just going to throw some steaks on the grill, man. I don't feel like making anything fancy tonight."

Paine glanced down at the dirty jeans he wore. "I don't have nothing else to wear."

"Don't worry. I'll pull out some sweats and a shirt for you. We'll throw your stuff in the washer with a load of mine. That way, they'll be clean for tomorrow."

"Okay."

They went upstairs, and Julio pointed out Paine's bedroom. He went in his room and grabbed some clothes. He tried very hard not to think about Paine wearing something of his next to all that lightly golden skin. He cringed as his erection pressed against his zipper, demanding it be let out to play.

He adjusted himself, wishing he had more room in his jeans. He couldn't take Paine to his bed, not now, and maybe never. It would take time for the wounds Paine'd received from his uncle to heal. Julio didn't want to push it, and did he want Paine because Paine was incredibly gorgeous and kind? Or did he want him because Paine needed a white knight, and Julio had an unhealthy need to rescue damsels in distress?

Not that Paine was a damsel or even needed to be rescued. There was nothing weak about the younger man, and nothing shattered beyond repair. He just needed time to learn to trust again. Julio planned to be there every step of the way, and when the time came, maybe Paine would look at him with desire in his eyes.

"Here you go."

He pushed open the door to the bedroom without knocking and froze. Paine jerked a pillow from the bed, but not before Julio got an eyeful of the man's groin. *Oh, wow!* Julio's throat went dry and he dropped his gaze to Paine's feet. But the image of Paine's semi-hard thick cock wouldn't get out of Julio's head.

"Ummm...sorry. I should've knocked." He held out the clothes before realizing Paine wasn't going to let go of the pillow to take them. "I'll just set them here."

Julio made sure the pile hit the dresser and didn't fall off before he raced from the room. *Shit.* What would Paine think of him barging in like the man didn't have any right to privacy? Would he think Julio was a pervert, just waiting for his chance to take advantage of him?

Standing in the middle of his room, Julio scrubbed his hands over his face and growled down at his own hard-on making his jeans tighter than they were just minutes ago. He stripped out of his clothes and went to his bathroom, where he started the shower and stared at his reflection in the mirror.

"Get a grip on yourself, Herendez. Paine's not fragile. I doubt he's going to freak out if he discovers you find him attractive. You can't do anything while the case is going on anyway. That'll give you time to get him to trust you."

He climbed under the hot water and let his head fall forward to rest his chin on his chest. Who was to say that, when things were back to normal, Paine wouldn't want a one-night stand or a fling to celebrate his freedom? Could Julio do that if it was what Paine wanted?

Sadly, no. Julio knew himself too well. His heart wasn't built for flings or one-night stands. He wanted relationships where they cooked dinner together and spent the evening curled up on the couch watching movies or playing video games. He liked the security of knowing he would be going out with the same person every weekend.

Julio washed quickly, not wanting Paine to get uncomfortable, waiting for Julio to finish. He cleaned up, dried off, and got dressed in record time. As he jogged down the stairs, he heard Paine's voice come from the kitchen. Easing down the hallway, he plastered himself against the wall. Yeah, eavesdropping wasn't very polite, even in his own house, but he wanted to know what Paine was thinking. The young man played his cards close to his vest and it was hard to get a read on him at times.

"Look at you, Miss Queenie. All comfortable and happy in this rather rag-tag pack. I do believe Julio has a tendency to adopt strays. What do you think?"

He could just imagine all three dogs sitting in the middle of the kitchen floor, staring up at Paine with matching "huh" expressions on their faces. Paine was right. He did collect strays. That's how he ended up with two ex-fighting dogs for pets, and an ex-rent boy as a best friend, plus said ex-rent boy's ex-heroin-addicted boyfriend.

"Do you think he sees me as a stray? As someone he needs to take care of? I don't want that. I mean, for the most part, I can take care of myself, though I'm not smart like most people. I need to learn how to read and write, guys. I know that'll help me, but what do I do about the future? When the case is over, Julio won't need to keep me around. I need to support myself and my cousins."

He heard the bang of a drawer. It sounded like Paine was searching for something.

"I don't know how to do nothing except take care of dogs. I don't even know how to make meth. Not that I'd start cooking that shit, but, see, I don't have any skills."

The scramble of nails on the hardwood floor alerted him to the fact one of the dogs was headed his way. He scooted back halfway down the hall before turning around and greeting Delilah. The look in her eyes almost made him think she knew he'd been listening. Of course, that was silly.

"Hey there, my beautiful lady. How are you?" He bent and rubbed her ears.

Delilah woofed at him before she turned and led him into the kitchen. Paine was chopping up lettuce when Julio entered.

"Did you want to take a shower?"

Paine shook his head. "Nah. I washed up in the sink."

Julio spied the drips of water still resting on the nape of Paine's neck and the wet spots on the long sleeve T-shirt Julio had given him.

"You can always take one before we go to bed." He moaned silently. No way did he want to think about Paine in a bed. "Glad you found the salad stuff. I'm going to fire up the grill and we'll get the meat cooking."

"Okay."

Dinner went well. Julio didn't burn anything, and Paine didn't seem too wigged out about staying at Julio's that night. There wasn't much conversation, though, and Julio tried to think of something to break the ice. They cleaned up the dishes, and Julio grabbed a beer from the refrigerator.

"Do you want a beer?"

Paine shook his head. "I don't drink. There had to be one clear head at home with my aunt being drunk off her ass all the time."

"Do you mind if I have a beer? I usually have one after dinner. Helps me relax after a stressful day." He held up the bottle.

"No. Go ahead. I'm not fanatical about it or anything. Figure you can probably hold your liquor better than Aunt Daisy."

"I hope so, and I rarely get drunk anymore. Did that in my college days and if I had a dollar for every time I found myself clinging to a toilet, I'd be a rich man. Not worth it anymore." He motioned to the back yard. "It's still nice outside. We could sit on the deck while the dogs play."

"Sounds good to me." Paine filled his glass with water and followed Julio.

They settled into chairs on the deck. Delilah, Samson, and Queenie played with their toys strewn across the yard. Julio rested his head on the back of his chair and stared up at the stars blinking in the velvet black sky.

"Did you always want to be an investigator?"

Paine's soft question almost disappeared under the night sounds, but Julio had focused intensely on the man next to him.

"No." Julio laughed. "I wanted to be a vet, but I figured out real quick I wasn't smart enough in math for that. Decided law enforcement might be something I could do. After graduating with a criminal justice degree, I went to the academy. Graduated from there, then I worked on the regular police force for a year before going to work for the Humane Society. I love my job most of the time."

Paine grunted, and Julio took that as a sign to keep talking.

"I investigate cruelty cases, and it breaks my heart when I see animals being abused. That's why I volunteered to go undercover to bust fight rings. Senseless brutality, that's all that is. Drives me crazy and makes me sick to my stomach."

"How'd you get your tattoo?"

Turning, he saw Paine touch just below the corner of his own eye in the same area where Julio's teardrop tattoo was.

"To the gangs, it means I killed a man, or spent time in prison. I got it before I went undercover the first time. I was a gangbanger looking to branch out. I needed something to give me some street cred. Had a police record and everything." Julio reached up and rubbed his finger over the tattoo. "To me personally, it's a symbol of all the animals I was too late to help. Those who died because of human arrogance."

Paine pursed his lips. "I thought it was because you'd killed someone."

"Well, Juke has killed people and served time in prison. He's a dangerous man who doesn't have any concern for anybody or anything. All he's interested in is what he can get." Julio shook his head and laughed. "If all those people who knew Juke could've seen me when I came home from a fight… I'd stand under the hottest water possible, scrubbing until I thought my skin would come off, trying to get the blood off me."

"But you never got near enough to the dogs to get blood on you," Paine pointed out.

"I know that, but it still felt like blood covered me. And God, if anyone followed me from one of those fights, they'd have seen me pull to the side of the road and puke my guts out." Julio leaned forward and braced his elbows on his knees, allowing his hands to dangle between them. "I hate fighting, whether it's dogs or cocks. It's so senseless and cruel."

He about jumped out of his chair when Paine laid his hand on his shoulder. He didn't look up or make a comment.

"I used to be like that. Uncle Caesar beat it out of me. I got to the point where I wouldn't watch them, but I could deal with the aftermath. The only reason Uncle would take me to those fights was to sell my ass if the opportunity presented itself."

"Paine, I have to ask this, and please don't feel like you need to answer."

"Okay." Paine didn't remove his hand.

"Are you gay?"

CHAPTER 6

The other man stiffened and started to pull away. Julio risked Paine freaking out by taking Paine's hand in his. He met Paine's worried gaze and tried to reassure him.

"I don't care if you are or not. I just wanted to know because I have to tell you. I'm really attracted to you and I don't want you to wig out on me if you notice my reaction to you."

Paine frowned, though his expression cleared when he dropped his gaze to Julio's groin and spied the tent his erection made of his sweats. Paine pulled away, and Julio groaned silently. Probably wasn't the smartest thing to do, but he couldn't keep it a secret anymore. He wasn't going to be able to do anything about the desire he felt for Paine, at least not until the case was over, but he thought Paine should know.

"I'm gay, I think."

"You think?" He studied the blond.

The laughter coming from Paine caused Julio to flinch. It was a bitter sound.

"How am I supposed to know when the only encounters with men I have are when some creepy bastard's fucking my mouth or ass because he gets off forcing someone?" Paine stood and paced, his arms wrapped tight around him. "That ain't the best way to figure out if I like guys or women. I mean, I ain't had a normal relationship with anyone, so I don't really know what I like."

Julio nodded and rested his face in his hands. "I figured as much."

"Glad you got it figured out, 'cause I don't. I like you, Julio. Hell, I had the hots for you when I thought you were some mean-ass drug dealer. How twisted does that make me?"

Julio climbed to his feet and approached Paine slowly, like he would a wild animal. He held his arms wide, giving Paine the option to move. When Paine stayed where he was, Julio embraced him.

Paine sighed and laid his head on Julio's shoulder, encircling Julio's waist with his arms. Julio rubbed his cheek over Paine's hair, breathing in the honest scent of sweat and musk.

"It doesn't make you twisted. It shows that you should trust your instincts a little. Something inside you said that I might not be as bad as I seemed. You knew the men and women who used you weren't doing it out of liking or desire for you personally. They used you because fucking someone who can't say no turns them on. It makes *them* twisted." Julio grimaced at the thought of what Paine went through so young.

"How will I know?" Paine's muffled question drifted up to Julio's ears.

As much as he hated saying it, Julio spoke up. "Once this case is over and your life is as back to normal as possible, we'll do some experiments to see how you react to other guys. Not only to see if you're attracted to them and to figure out if you're really gay, but I want you to be sure you desire me for the right reasons and not because I'm helping you escape a terrible situation. Did you find Pedro attractive?"

"Yeah. He's pretty hot."

"Then I'd say it's a pretty good chance you're gay, but we can take it slow."

Paine eased back a little so their gazes could meet. The small furrow between Paine's eyebrows told Julio the man was confused. Julio made a decision. He stepped away, tugging Paine along with him until they reached one of the chairs. After dropping down into it, he encouraged Paine to curl up on his lap. He hoped Paine would ignore the hard length of flesh poking at his ass.

While Paine seemed a little hesitant to join him, Julio didn't think it was because of the obvious sign of Julio's lust. More than likely Paine didn't know how to accept comfort or affection from anyone. Soon they were entangled, arms and legs, in the chair. Paine's head lay on Julio's chest, and Julio absorbed not only Paine's warmth, but the beat of the man's heart into his body.

"I have a white knight complex. At least, that's what Pedro tells me. I see a person in need and I have to help them in any way I can. It's not that I think you are weak or so fragile that you can't do it on your own." Julio chuckled softly. "God knows, you're one of the strongest people I've ever met. To keep on going after everything you've had to deal with. Amazing."

"I ain't that special," Paine mumbled, obviously uncomfortable with Julio's praise.

"I think you are. What my worry is, and this is purely selfish on my part, is that you're attracted to me because I'm the first person who was nice to you."

Paine started to say something, and Julio tightened his embrace to make him stop.

"Don't say it's not. We don't know for sure. I've already broken protocol a couple times with this case. I don't want to screw anything else up. So we can't go any further than where we are now until after the trial." Julio took a deep breath and plunged on. "I really like you, Paine, more than anyone I've ever been attracted to before. I'd hate to rush you into a relationship, only to find out later it was just gratitude that made you take me into your bed. I don't want you to be unhappy or feel obligated. I'm not your uncle, expecting you to repay me for anything I do for you."

He stopped and the night sounds poured into the void left by the absence of his voice. Tension seeped into his muscles as he worried about what Paine would say. Paine started shaking, and Julio panicked. Had he caused Paine to cry? God, he didn't want to upset the man that much.

Paine pushed away from him, and he loosened his grip. Looking down, he noticed that laughter shook Paine, not tears. The bright smile gracing Paine's plump lips beamed from his eyes as well. Julio didn't think he'd ever seen a man so gorgeous in all his life.

"Silly man," Paine said fondly. He patted Julio's cheek, leaving Julio in shock at the affection in Paine's touch. "I'm grateful to you for having the guts to arrest my uncle and saving us all from him. I freely admit that, but I ain't the kind of guy to sleep with you 'cause of that. I don't plan on ever using my body to repay favors again."

Julio's pride in Paine grew at the man's words. "I'm glad to hear that."

"A part of me wants to drag you off to a bed. Yours or mine, it don't matter. I want you buried deep in me." Paine held up his hand to stop Julio from speaking. "You're right. It ain't good for you and me to start something now. I got issues needing to be worked on, and you got this case to take care of."

Reaching out, Julio cradled Paine's face in his hands. "How did you get to be so wise?"

Paine shrugged, a faint lift to one corner of his mouth. "Don't have much to do but think while I'm nursing a sick dog. I know you ain't gonna hurt me, but I have to be able to trust other people besides you."

"Would you be willing to talk to a therapist about all of this?"

"I don't got money to pay for one of those."

Paine's gaze dropped to Julio's chest, even though he couldn't move his head since Julio still held him. Julio smiled and gave Paine a little shake to make him look at him.

"There are places where you can go and get help without it costing you anything or very little. We can talk to Pedro about it. He's likely to know about them."

"I have to pay the man back for letting me crash at his place." Paine bit his bottom lip as he thought.

Julio rubbed his thumb over the abused flesh. "Don't worry too much about it. Pedro was happy to help, and he won't sweat you about paying. Take your time and give him what you can."

Paine agreed and snuggled close again. Julio was glad Paine didn't argue about making sure Pedro got all the money Paine thought he owed him. Julio knew his friend, and Pedro wouldn't be happy about accepting the money. He'd talk to Pedro in the morning.

"How did you get to be friends with Pedro?"

"Are you wondering what a high school guidance counselor and an undercover cop have in common?"

"Yeah. You don't go to the schools very often, do you?"

He snorted. "Not if I can help it. To be honest, I arrested Pedro for prostitution the first year I was on the regular police force."

"No shit?" Paine leaned back and eyed him.

"I'm not kidding. Wouldn't know it to look at him, but Pedro's had a rough life. You'll have to ask him about it sometime. I'm sure he'd be able to relate to what you've gone through."

It wouldn't be a bad thing for Pedro and Paine to talk about their mutual pasts. Paine needed to see there were others who had gone through what he had and turned out to have good lives.

"How long have he and Santo been together?"

"They hooked up right out of high school. Santo was a heroin addict, and Pedro sold himself to keep them from living on the streets. My arresting Pedro got help for both of them and so far, they've made a go of it. Santo's out of the country three or four months out of the year, but it seems to work for them. Hell, I can't judge. I've never been in a serious relationship."

Paine shifted and his ass brushed over Julio's cock, drawing a gasp from him. Paine froze, but Julio stroked his hands down the younger man's shoulders to let him know it was okay. Settling as close as he possibly could get, Paine nuzzled Julio's chin.

"Why not?"

"Why not what?" Julio forgot what they'd been talking about.

"Why haven't you had a relationship? You like playing the field?"

Julio laughed so hard he almost knocked Paine off his lap. "Oh, hell, no. I'm so not a player. I hate one-night stands. I did a few of them while in college, but figured out quickly I don't like going home with a different guy every night."

"Are you a homebody?" Paine trailed his hand up and down Julio's arm.

"Yep. Never had a home of my own when I was a kid. My family moved around a lot. My parents were illegals and had to get work wherever they could. I was born in the States along with my sister, so we got our citizenship. Didn't matter for my parents. We'd stay in a place for a month or two before moving somewhere else. It's surprising I managed to graduate from high school at all."

He looked out over his backyard, smiling at the sight of the three dogs curled in a big pile sleeping. "I was so proud the minute I signed the mortgage on this place. It's all mine and I love spending time here, though it's not nearly as fun as sitting out here like this with you."

"And the dogs?"

"Yeah. The dogs keep me company when I get home from work, plus I see them and they remind me why I do it. Seeing them run around the house and the yard makes me feel like I'm doing a good job."

"You are."

Paine wiggled until he straddled Julio's thighs. Julio gripped Paine's hips, trying not to whimper as Paine leaned forward to press a kiss to Julio's lips. He swept his tongue over the seam of Paine's mouth, demanding entrance.

*   *   *

Holy cow, Julio could kiss. BB's eyes drifted closed as Julio took control of the kiss. It didn't matter to him since this was the first real kiss he'd ever gotten. None of the people who paid to screw him wanted to kiss him. Maybe it was too intimate or personal, but BB didn't see how it could be anymore intimate than having some guy's cock in his ass.

He braced his hands on Julio's shoulders and angled his head, drawing Julio's tongue into his mouth. They dueled and stroked, teasing each other. BB moaned deep in his throat as Julio tugged him closer until their groins rubbed together.

Shit. He jerked at the way his cock swelled just from kissing and the slight touches. Letting his hands slide down the front of Julio's T-shirt, he tested the muscled chest with his fingers. Julio moved forward a little and jerked his shirt off, revealing the entire expense of his broad chest. BB plucked Julio's nipples, twisting slightly, while Julio groaned in his mouth.

"Paine, we need to stop," Julio said after they'd kissed and played for a few minutes.

"I don't want to," he protested.

"I know, baby, but I can't take much more of this without taking you, and we can't do that. Not now."

Julio eased him down until their bodies pressed tight together, but his hands soothed BB instead of excited him. Their breathing calmed, along with their heartbeats. By the time his desire died down, the night air had gotten chilly and the dogs gathered around them.

He climbed off Julio and held out his hand to help the man stand.

"It's time for bed," Julio muttered. "God, I'd like nothing more than to carry you up to my bedroom, but I have to exercise some restraint. You're a witness in a case I'm working on. Everything about you calls to me and I can see spending a lot of time with you."

BB blushed and bent to scratch Queenie's ears. "I understand. You told me we couldn't get busy or nothing right now, but I wanted to know what it's like to kiss you."

Julio chuckled. "Thank you. I hope it was all you wanted and that you'd like to do it again later."

Straightening, BB met Julio's gaze and nodded. "Let's make a pact. When this case is over, and my uncle ain't around no more, we'll investigate these feelings between us. See if we fit together or if it's just the excitement of the case."

He didn't back away when Julio invaded his personal space. He wrapped his arms around Julio's shoulders and accepted Julio's kiss willingly. They nibbled on each other's lips, and he sucked on Julio's tongue. BB didn't know how long they stood there kissing before one of the dogs nudged his leg.

One more quick peck and he stepped away. Julio licked his lips and heaved a heavy breath. "This is going to be a long couple of months."

BB agreed. "Yeah, it is, but you know what? I've never looked forward to nothing in my life. Now I will and I'm getting the feeling it's gonna be like Christmas for me."

"Christmas has always been my favorite holiday."

The dogs and BB followed Julio back into the house. Julio locked the door and set the alarm before they headed upstairs. Julio left him and Queenie at BB's bedroom door and continued down the hallway to the other room.

BB brushed his teeth, using one of the new toothbrushes he found in the bathroom cabinet. After finishing, he crawled under the blankets. Queenie whined from the floor at the side of the bed. He rolled over and stared at her for a moment.

"I have to find out if it's okay first."

He opened the door and padded to Julio's door where he knocked.

"Come in."

"Hey, is it okay if Queenie sleeps on the bed with me?"

Peering around the edge of the door, he grinned at the sight of Julio sitting up bed with Samson and Delilah curled up on the blankets next to him.

"Guess that answers my question. Good thing you don't have no one to share your bed. There wouldn't be room for them."

Julio's intense gaze raked BB from head to toe. "For the right guy, I'd make room in my bed."

BB's heart skipped a beat and he swallowed hard. "I look forward to sharing your bed with the dogs. We might need to get a king-sized bed for all of us."

"We'll keep that in mind. 'Night, Paine."

"'Night, Julio."

By the time he got back to his room, Queenie had already climbed up on the bed. She curled up on the right side, her head resting on the pillow.

"Just make yourself at home, Your Majesty."

She sneezed in disdain, and he chuckled. After stripping off his clothes, he crawled under the blankets again. He turned off the lamp on the nightstand. Snuggling deeper into the covers and the mattress, he relaxed, letting all the tension in his muscles go.

He and Queenie were safe at Julio's. Uncle Caesar or his business partners weren't going to get him. He couldn't help but worry about reprisals because he was ratting out his family. Yet, except for his cousins, he didn't really consider Uncle Caesar and Aunt Daisy as real family. They might share his blood, but they didn't give a damn about him or the girls.

Maybe he should feel bad about helping put his uncle in jail. Did it make him a horrible person that he was glad his uncle would be locked up? And he hoped Uncle Caesar would get his ass kicked in prison. The man needed to learn what it was like to be the victim and have someone bigger or meaner than him in control.

Queenie snorted in her sleep, and BB laughed softly. *Silly dog.* He laid his hand on her back and let his eyes drift close. Tomorrow would arrive, no matter how much he wished they could stay here, wrapped in blankets in a house where he felt safe and cared for.

But Katie and Betsy needed the same opportunity to feel like someone would protect them, so he hoped Julio got permission to take them away from his aunt. More than anything, he wanted his cousins to act like teenagers instead of ghosts. Every child deserved the chance to be one.

CHAPTER 7

Julio paced, his hands stuck in his pockets. Where the hell was Paine? He'd promised to be there and Paine didn't seem the type to break his word.

Time continued to tick and Julio thought about the fast-talking he'd done to convince Emerson that Paine needed to be there when they removed the girls from the house. He threaded his way through the piles of garbage. Trash filled the front yard and the stench wafting from the trailer tempted Julio to gag. How could anyone live like that?

Hell, the kennels and even the meth lab were cleaner than this place. That was saying a lot because addicts weren't known for being particularly neat. The dogs the DEA took from the meth property had been delivered to the shelter, so that could be a reason why Paine was late.

Glancing over at the trailer, he studied the windows and doors. Paine had warned them that his aunt probably had a gun in there and she knew how to shoot, even though no one had seen any movement since they arrived at the property.

Great. Just what they needed—some drunk woman shooting at them while they tried to take her daughters from her. That would go over well on the evening news. Julio tapped his vest and prayed it wouldn't be put to use today.

Paine's beat-up truck pulled to a stop behind one of the police cars. He hopped out, and Julio bit his lip to keep from moaning out loud. Christ, could the guy look any better? Baggy khaki cargo pants hid that firm ass from view, but Julio knew what it felt like pressed against his groin. A tight sleeveless T-shirt lovingly hugged Paine's lean chest, exposing in glorious detail every muscle in the man's stomach. The guy was ripped, probably from taking care of the dogs all day.

He watched Paine weave his way through the crowd of police officers and social workers as he headed toward Julio. Paine stopped a foot away and held out his hand.

"Sorry, I'm late. I wanted to make sure the two dogs brought in were all right. They don't seem too bothered by the tranquilizers."

Julio shook Paine's hand and smiled. "No worries. I figured it had something to do with the dogs."

He let go and turned to look at the house. "We haven't seen any movement since we arrived. Are you sure they'll be here?"

"Aunt Daisy should be drunk off her ass by now." Paine checked his watch. "Katie and Betsy haven't gone to school in a year or two. They don't do well in a crowd."

"Right." Julio thought for a second and rearranged the plan for getting the girls. He gestured, and the others gathered around him. "Okay, this is how we're going to handle it. I want one of the social workers to come to the door with Paine and me. The rest of you spread out. Maybe a couple of you should go around back, just in case the woman decides to leave. Be careful, though; we have reason to believe there's at least one gun in the house and the woman knows how to use it."

Getting affirmative nods from everyone, Julio motioned them to take their places. A petite Hispanic woman joined him and Paine at the foot of the front steps. Julio looked her over and nodded. She wasn't wearing a vest and neither was Paine, but Julio intended to be standing in front of them, in case Aunt Daisy used the gun.

"Are you ready?"

Both Paine and the woman nodded. Julio started up the steps. Before he got to the top one, the door opened and a skinny brunette girl burst out.

"BB, that you?" She launched herself off the steps into Paine's arms.

"Yeah, it's me, Katie girl. I've come to get you."

Julio touched the social worker's arm and they eased a few steps away. Julio kept a sharp eye out for Aunt Daisy, but he didn't want to upset the girl anymore than she was.

"Momma left, BB, after Daddy went away. Bets and I woke up and she wasn't here no more."

"Damn," Julio swore softly.

The girls had been on their own for at least a week-and-a-half. Why hadn't any one come to check on them sooner?

"Why didn't you come back?" Katie looked up at Paine, tears dripping down her face. "I never thought you'd abandon us, too, BB."

Paine's expression broke Julio's heart. It was obvious Paine thought he'd let his cousins down, even more than he had when he lived with them.

"I'm truly sorry, Katie girl. I thought Aunt Daisy would stick with you. I should've known the witch would take off at the first sign of trouble." Paine let Katie go and brushed back the hair from her face. "Where's Betsy? We're leaving here and going to a different house. A better one with actual running water."

"Will it be warm? Can we have our own rooms?" Katie babbled as she took Paine's hand and dragged him up the steps to the door.

"Wait," Julio said, moving to keep them from going in.

Katie gasped and shrunk close to Paine, her eyes wide with fear. So she wasn't afraid of Paine, but of every other male in the area once she realized they were there. Freezing, Julio shot Paine a quick glance. Paine wrapped an arm around Katie's shoulders and lifted her chin with his other hand.

"Katie, this is my friend, Julio Herendez. He's here to help us. We'll be staying at his house. He won't hurt you, honey."

The look on her face told them she didn't believe Paine, and Julio was fine with that. He understood it took time to build trust, especially with a damaged creature like Katie. Betsy would be just as ill treated and would have to be handled with kid gloves.

"Hello, Katie. I'm happy you and your sister will be coming to stay with me. Paine will be there, as well as my dogs. They'll love having someone to play with them while I'm at work."

He kept his voice low, like he was talking to one of the fighting dogs. Abused creatures reacted to loud noises and violence. They didn't know how to handle kindness and it made them curious. More than likely, Katie would react the same way.

"Dogs?"

"Yeah, honey. Julio's got two pits like ours, and Queenie's staying with him. Remember how I took you out one time to meet her? You'd like to see Queenie again, wouldn't you?"

She nodded, but her eyes darted over to where Julio stood. The social worker moved then and caught Katie's attention. Katie shrank even more, giving Julio another clue into what happened behind the doors of this house. Aunt Daisy not only let her husband sell her daughters, she obviously abused them herself.

"I'm Maria, Katie. May I come in with you and Paine to get Betsy? We'll have to pack some clothes for you two as well." Maria's words were gentle, but Katie nearly vibrated with tension.

"Come on, Katie girl. We gotta get Betsy and head out. After we get you cleaned up and fed, maybe you'd like to go and see the dogs with me."

Paine got them moving and, once they were inside, Julio stood by the front door while the others went to the girls' room. Julio breathed through his mouth as the smell was ten times worse inside. He didn't touch anything, but still thought he might just burn his clothes when they were done there.

He peered into the living room and almost lost what little was in his stomach. Cockroaches crawled over rotten food sitting on the floor. Liquor bottles lay scattered all across the room, covering every surface. Dirt seemed to be the color scheme for every piece of furniture in the room. *How could anyone survive in a place like this?*

A tiny sound drew his attention to a small closet farther inside the trailer. He cautiously moved toward it. The door was opened a crack and Julio had a feeling he knew what or who was in there. He heard Paine and Katie yelling for Betsy down the hallway. Resting his hand on his gun because it didn't hurt to be cautious, he widened the crack in the door with his foot.

He peered into the minuscule area and didn't see anything at first. A whimper brought his gaze to a pile of blankets in the corner. Something moved beneath them and, as much as Julio wanted to pull the fabric back and reveal who was under there, he inched back until he stood in the hallway.

"Paine, Katie, I think I know where Betsy is. Can you two come here?" he called.

"Shit."

Paine raced down the hall, with Katie right behind him. Julio pointed to the closet and met the inquiring gaze of Maria. Grimacing, he shook his head. She closed her eyes and sighed.

"I completely agree," Julio murmured as she joined him by the front door.

"Oh, Bets, what're you doing in here?"

Paine crouched down and tugged the blankets away. The shocked expression on his face alerted Julio that there might problems. As much as he wanted to go and envelope the man in a hug, he stayed where he was, choosing not to frighten Katie over comforting Paine. He'd do that later when there weren't so many people around.

Maria gasped as Paine drew Betsy from the closet. Where Katie was skinny, Betsy was skin and bones. It looked like the girl hadn't eaten for weeks. In a way, she looked like a concentration camp survivor. There were bruises all over her body and she was naked.

Julio averted his eyes and started unfastening his vest. "Paine, here use my shirt. I don't think she'd want anything from this house touching her."

He stripped off his top long-sleeve shirt, grateful for the T-shirt he wore underneath, and held it out.

"Take it from him, Katie. It's all right. Julio won't hurt you."

The shirt was tugged from his hand. Julio's gaze connected with Maria's and he saw the tears welling up in hers. *Shit on a cracker.* This was worse than anything Julio could have imagined. Why did people do this to each other? Why were there some humans out there who didn't have an ounce of decency in their body?

Reaching out, he patted Maria's arm. "Why don't you go outside and wait for us? Nothing's going to happen to them now. Not if I have any say in the matter. Call the hospital and let them know we're bringing the girls in."

She nodded and left. Julio kept his eyes trained on the wall, trying not to react to the whimpers and soft cries coming from behind him. A light touch to his hand made him jump and he looked to his right, spying Katie standing next to him.

"We're ready." She swallowed hard, and he could see the courage it took for her to talk to him.

"Okay." He shot a quick glance over at Paine who held Betsy in his arms. "We're going to have to take them to the hospital."

Paine frowned and looked down at Betsy, curled up with her face hidden against his chest. The teenager almost disappeared in Julio's shirt.

"I know, honey, but we can't take a chance on them getting sick or something. It's the right thing to do. I'll make sure they don't separate you."

When Paine nodded, Julio felt like he'd won the lottery. It was hell being the only person Paine truly trusted, but Julio wasn't going to risk losing that trust. He'd walk through the fires of hell to insure all of them were safe.

"Take her out to my car. You and the girls can sit in back and I'll drive. No one will stop you."

Julio shoved open the door, and Paine walked out with Katie almost in his hip pocket. Julio gestured for everyone to get out of the way. The crowd parted like the Red Sea, allowing Paine to pass by without anyone accidentally touching either girl. After unlocking the car, Julio stopped and grabbed hold of Smith.

"I'm going to the hospital with them. I want pictures of everything in that trailer. We'll bring the bastard and his wife up on child abuse charges as well."

The grim faces surrounding him encouraged him. There wouldn't be any short cuts or carelessness at the property. Every man and woman there wanted to nail Caesar Addison's hide to the wall because of his daughters.

"Oh, and see if you can find out where the mother went. She's not getting away with this." He started toward the car, but stopped and turned. "You're going to want gloves and face masks to go in there. It's disgusting."

"Should we pack anything for the girls?" one of the female agents asked.

"Let me check."

Julio jogged over to the car and tapped on the window. Paine rolled it down.

"Is there anything in that house the girls might want to keep? Clothes? A personal item?"

Katie listened and shook her head when Paine looked at her. "We didn't have nothing. Momma wouldn't spend money on nothing but liquor or cigarettes. There's just some clothes. They ain't nothing but rags, so you could burn the whole thing to ashes for all we care."

Julio saw how Katie kept her hand on Betsy's back.

"All right. I'll let them know."

He informed the agent in charge and climbed behind the wheel. After starting the car and putting it in drive, he slung his arm over the back of the seats and turned to check behind him. His eyes met Paine's bright blue ones. His chest tightened at the pain and rage swirling in Paine's gaze.

Julio clenched his fist, knowing he would have to go hit the punching bag at the gym and work through his anger. He couldn't spend any time with Paine or the girls with all the rage boiling inside him. He started when Paine rested his hand on his.

"It'll be okay. Just get us to the hospital."

He nodded and got them headed toward the city. He ignored the whispers and whimpers from the backseat. Julio walled off his emotions, burying them deep in his soul. It wouldn't help the trio if he broke down as well. There would be a time when he was alone where he could curl up in a ball and whimper like Betsy did.

*   *   *

BB stared at the back of Julio's head, reading all the signs of fury in the man's body. He dropped his chin to nuzzle the top of Betsy's head. Under the smell of urine, shit, and dirt, he managed to catch a whiff of Julio's cologne. It came from the shirt Betsy wore to cover her nakedness.

Why was Betsy hiding in the closet naked? Where had those fresh bruises come from if Aunt Daisy hadn't been around for two weeks?

"Katie, did anyone come see you after Aunt Daisy left?"

Katie shook her head. "No, but Big T dropped Bets off a couple days ago. It's just been me until then."

"Big T?"

"One of Daddy's friends. He took Betsy the night before Daddy got arrested. Wasn't supposed to keep her so long, but I guess with Daddy not around, he didn't see no need to bring her back right away." Katie stroked a hand over Betsy's back. "I thought I'd never seen neither one of you again."

"I'm sorry, Katie. I should've come back a lot sooner. I just thought your momma'd stick around. I never thought she'd run like she did. She might suck as a mother, but you're her kids. She should've taken care of you."

Guilt swamped him as he thought of what the girls suffered in the week or so it took him to come back for them. It didn't matter they had to wait for the court to come up with a subpoena or whatever to remove the girls. He should have driven over and grabbed them.

"It's okay, BB. We don't blame you none. Heck, if we could leave, we would've. Nothing here to hold us down, you know. Family don't mean nothing except blood. You came back for us. It don't matter when you did. You didn't forget about us like Momma and Daddy did." Katie leaned her cheek on his shoulder, but her gaze never left Julio's back. "And you brought someone to help us."

How did she know Julio wouldn't hurt her? Of course, that didn't mean she was going to go running into the man's arms. Maybe someday she'd be willing to accept him into their lives. BB heaved a mental sigh.

More baggage to carry around with him. No longer could he be concerned with just himself and the dogs. He had two girls depending on him to make their world better. He hadn't thought about that. Would Julio want to hitch his wagon to BB's anchor? No man in his right mind would disrupt his calm life by starting a relationship with him.

"Does he really have dogs?" Her dull brown eyes brightened a little at the thought of dogs.

"Yes, he has two dogs that are like ours. Samson and Delilah. Queenie's staying there as well until I can find a place for us to live."

"We're staying at his place?"

"Once the doctors get done checking you and Betsy out, we'll be going to his house."

Katie pursed her lips, worry clear on her face.

"Don't worry. Julio likes kids, but he won't touch you in any way. He doesn't think that's right. Besides, Julio likes guys. Adult guys."

Her eyes landed on him and she clutched at his arm. "He don't hurt you, does he?"

"No, Katie girl. Julio isn't that type of man. He doesn't hurt people. He's a police officer for animals. He tries to keep them safe." He rubbed his cheek on Betsy's hair, sure the younger girl listened to their conversation. "Julio's going to help me keep you safe. You won't go back to Aunt Daisy or Uncle Caesar ever. No one will ever hurt you again."

She didn't look convinced, but BB figured they had all the time in the world to make her see not every man was like her daddy.

"Paine."

He met Julio's gaze in the rearview mirror.

"We're at the hospital. I had Maria call ahead, so they know who we're bringing in. Why don't you take Betsy and Katie in while I park the car? Explain to them that you aren't to be separated. If they have a problem with it, I'll talk to them when I get in."

"All right."

Julio climbed out and opened the car door for him. He noticed how Julio stepped back in order not to crowd the girls. He stumbled getting out, and Julio caught him under the arm, holding him up until he found his balance again.

"Thanks. Come on, Katie."

He led the way into the hospital, where a nurse met them. She was older, shorter than Katie, with white hair. A grandmotherly type. Maybe they figured she wouldn't be as scary to them as a younger woman or man would be.

"My name's Sally. If you'll follow me, I'll set you all up in a room and a doctor will be around soon."

BB let Katie walk in front of him, while keeping an eye on all those around him. The hastily disguised looks of horror on the medical people's faces set his teeth on edge, yet they didn't mean anything by it, he knew. Most of them were good-hearted people horrified by what had happened to Katie and Betsy.

"Here's your room." Sally bustled around, tugging down the blankets and pulling out two gowns. "Girls, I'd like you to put these on, and the doctor will be in soon. You can have a seat right there, sir."

BB set Betsy on the bed and sat in the chair close to the side of it. "I'm going to close my eyes. Katie, why don't you change into the gown before helping Betsy? Just let me know when I can open my eyes."

"Okay."

The sound of clothing rustling told him that they were getting undressed. God, he hoped Julio didn't walk in right then. A few minutes went by before he felt someone touch his hand.

"You can look now, BB."

Opening his eyes, his gaze landed on Betsy and tears welled up. He dropped to his knees in front of her and took her hands in his. She stared at the wall behind him with blank blue eyes, so much like his own at certain times in his life. She'd been a frail child to begin with, not healthy or robust like Katie or him. Betsy didn't jerk away from him. She didn't move at all, almost like nothing around her registered in her brain.

"What did they do to you, baby girl?"

BB fought the urge to growl, knowing it would frighten both girls. Katie laid one hand on his shoulder and one on Betsy's knee, connecting them in their damaged circle. BB met Katie's tear-filled look. Katie knew there was something more than physically wrong with her sister.

Katie was tough, having dealt with being forced to do things no child should. She was broken and scarred, but she wasn't going to let her daddy destroy her. She wasn't going to let him have that satisfaction. BB knew all that from having talked to the girl before all of the shit started happening to Uncle Caesar. There was steel in her backbone and hatred in her heart for her daddy.

A knock sounded on the door and BB stood, moving to stand between the door and the girls. Julio looked in and saw him there. The small smile tilting the corners of Julio's mouth touched something inside BB, making him wish he could throw himself into the man's arms and hide away from the entire fucking world.

"The doctor would like to come in now."

"Are you okay with that, Katie?"

Katie took a deep breath and straightened her shoulders. She took Betsy's hand in hers and nodded. Julio stepped aside and the doctor entered. She was tall for a girl, maybe around five-nine and slender. A pair of glasses hid her green eyes and there was a softness in her features. Some hidden tension eased in BB. This woman wouldn't hurt the girls. She struck BB as the type of person who would cut off her own arm before she caused another person pain.

Sally slipped into the room behind them. "Katie, Betsy, and Paine, this is Doctor Paula St. Martine. She just wants to make sure there isn't anything wrong with you." Julio grimaced at that. "Anything wrong that you should stay at the hospital to take care of. You've already met Sally."

Betsy vocalized some protest, but BB didn't know if it was about the doctor touching her or about staying at the hospital.

"Good to meet you, ma'am. This is Katie and Betsy, my cousins. I'm BB—" He stopped.

He couldn't allow himself to think like that anymore. He wasn't Butt Boy. BB wasn't strong or brave. He was a whipping boy for his uncle and his associates.

Paine was strong and would protect those who couldn't protect themselves. He looked at Julio who gave him a wink of encouragement.

"I'm Paine Addison."

"Nice to meet you, Paine. Katie and Betsy, I have to check and make sure you aren't hurt worse than we can see. I have some questions to ask you and please be as truthful as you can."

Katie looked nervously at Paine. "Paine?" she asked.

"It's okay, Katie. Julio and me will be right here the whole time. The doc won't do nothing that you don't want. Just try to answer her as best you can. She can't help take the pain away if you don't tell her."

"The pain won't ever go away," Betsy whispered, her eyes still boring into the wall over Katie's shoulder.

"You're right, Betsy. There are some pains that'll never go away," Julio said gently. "But the doctor can help stop your body from hurting, and time will dull the memories."

Katie trembled, but she nodded. "Okay. You can look me over first. Bets, you watch and see that she won't do nothing to me."

Betsy blinked and turned her head slightly, keeping the doctor and Katie in her peripheral vision. Paine inched over to where Julio stood and shifted his weight so he leaned on Julio. He relaxed a little when Julio's hand rested on his hip.

Doctor St. Martine spoke softly, and while Katie eyed her suspiciously, she let the doctor check her over. Betsy didn't say a word, just did what the doctor told her like a robot. After an hour and several questions Paine wished he hadn't heard the answer to, Doctor St. Martine finished up. She tossed her gloves in the wastebasket and came over to where Paine and Julio stood.

"Can I talk to you outside?" She gestured for Paine to follow her.

Paine hesitated, and Julio glanced at him before looking at Katie.

"Katie, would it be all right if I stayed in the room with you? I'll stand next to the door and it'll stay open, so you can see Paine while he talks to the doctor. If you want, Sally will stay in here as well."

God, what a great guy Julio was. He knew Katie should be the one making the decision whether Julio stayed in the room or not. Too much control of their lives had been taken from them. From that moment on, they would always be able to decide for themselves what happened to them.

"It's okay. You can go and talk to her, BB…I mean Paine. Julio can stay here with us." Katie settled on the bed and embraced Betsy.

"Thanks, Katie."

Doctor St. Martine escorted Paine out into the hallway, far enough way so the girls couldn't hear, but not out of their sight.

CHAPTER 8

Doctor St. Martine cleared her throat and rubbed her hands on her lab coat. "I wasn't given much information when I was assigned this case. They just told me it was neglect and there were two girls."

Paine watched as the doctor paced a little bit in each direction, never getting too far from him. He saw the woman's rage shaking her. He wanted to reach out and grab the doctor, telling her it would be okay because nothing bad would ever happen to those girls again. Of course, the damage had already been done to them.

"I'm assuming you didn't do any of that to them."

"What? Hell, no. I wouldn't do anything to kids to begin with and what was done to them makes my stomach sick." Paine shook his head. "I'm hoping Julio's friends in the police department can do something to punish the bastards who would this to people."

"I hope they fry them," Dr. St. Martine muttered.

"You and me both, Doc." Paine looked over his shoulder into the room. Katie still held Betsy and they rocked back and forth. "Are they okay, Doc? I mean physically. Emotional and mental scars will take longer to heal and you can't really help with those anyway."

The doctor threw her shoulders back and unclenched her jaw. "Aside from the bruises and malnutrition, they're fine. They just need time to heal. I couldn't find any internal injuries. Betsy probably had broken ribs at some point, but those have healed and I don't think they cause her any trouble. Katie appears to be fine physically, just severely underweight."

"I did the best for them that I could, but I haven't been around for a week or so. Trying to get my own screwed-up life in order. So some of the blame for their condition is on my shoulders." Paine dropped his head forward and stared at the floor, guilt swelling inside him again.

"None of the blame lies on your shoulders, unless you were the one selling these girls." Doctor St. Martine poked Paine in the chest. "You need to work on your mental health before you can help your cousins."

"I know and I'm getting help." He gestured toward Julio. "Julio's looking into some places I can go for counseling. I don't have much money right now."

"Hmmm…I might be able to help you with that. Give me your number and I'll call you with some names."

"I don't have a phone no more. It got disconnected when my uncle was arrested."

"Give her my number, Paine, and I'll get the message to you," Julio suggested from where he stood in the doorway.

"Okay."

Paine repeated Julio's cell number to the doctor, who wrote it down and stuck it in her pocket.

"Thanks. Sally took pictures of the bruises, and I'll write up a report. We'll send their files over to child services and the police. I'm sure there'll be enough evidence to throw the book at your uncle and aunt."

"If we can find Aunt Daisy, that'd be great. I'd like to make her pay for what she didn't do for Katie and Betsy."

"And you." Julio stepped up behind him and laid his hand on Paine's shoulder.

He shook his head. "Nah. I don't matter. Just some bastard dumped by his mother on relatives who didn't want him. Brought them all nothing but pain and trouble. But Katie and Betsy? My aunt's got no excuse for treating her own children that way. I hope she burns in hell when she gets there."

Neither Julio nor Dr. St. Martine said anything to counteract the bitterness in Paine's voice. In his mind, he knew what he said wasn't totally true. He did matter and shouldn't have been sold either, but he'd always heard that being a throwaway kid made him less a part of the family.

"We should get going and take the girls home, so they can clean up and eat."

"We don't have any clothes for them," he pointed out after saying good-bye to the doctor.

Julio frowned. "I'd hate taking them to the store. People would stare and that's not the best way to start out a new life."

Maryanne walked off the elevator right then and held up a set of keys. "I brought Paine's truck over."

Relief shone on Julio's face. "Great. Paine, why don't you take Katie and Betsy home? I'll grab Maryanne and take her to the store with me. She can help me pick out some clothes. When the girls are better, we can take them to get more stuff."

Maryanne looked like she wanted to protest, but one glance from Julio and she kept her mouth shut.

"Sounds good to me."

Sally came bustling back to them with her arms full of fabric. "Here…I brought each of the girls a set of scrubs. We can't let them leave the hospital wearing those filthy clothes or your shirt."

Paine accepted the scrubs and took them into the room. After laying them on the bed, he tapped Katie on the shoulder.

"Hey, Katie girl, here's some clothes for you and Betsy. They're clean, though they might be a little big. I'm taking you to Julio's house, where you can get cleaned up and eat. Julio and his friend Maryanne are stopping by a store to pick up some new outfits for you."

Katie nodded and slipped off the mattress. Paine left as she unfolded the first shirt. He closed the door behind him, not shutting it completely. He moved into Julio's personal space and the man cupped his face in his hands. Their gazes joined, and Paine absorbed the concern he saw in Julio's eyes.

"Are you okay?"

He shrugged. "Not sure yet. Too much happening and still needs to happen. Probably around midnight tonight, I'll break down."

"I'll be there to hold you if you need it." Julio didn't look around. He leaned forward and pressed his lips to Paine's.

Paine gripped Julio's hips and found the bottom of the T-Shirt to slip his fingers under the hem. He stroked Julio's warm skin underneath his touch, while he nibbled on Julio's bottom lip.

The sound of footsteps approaching behind him broke Paine away from Julio. As much as he wanted to remain lost in Julio's embrace, he understood he had to continue to be strong for a while longer. At some time in the future, he would reach his breaking point and Julio would be there to pick up the pieces. A hospital wasn't really the best place for a complete breakdown unless it was a mental ward.

Maryanne stood with her back to them, and Paine realized he'd forgotten she was there. Looking over at Julio, he noticed the man didn't seem too worried about Maryanne seeing them kiss.

"Paine, we're ready to go."

Katie and Betsy stepped into the corridor, holding hands. Paine crouched down, peering into Betsy's face. The younger girl blinked and finally focused on him.

"Hey there, Bets, you ready to come home with me? You can take a shower, put on clean clothes, and eat something. You're safe now, and no one will ever touch you again in anger or wanting to cause you pain." He took her hands and stared intensely at her, praying she believed him.

She blinked slowly again before nodding once. Paine wanted to jump for joy at her response, but he managed to keep control of his emotions.

"Do you need help walking to the truck?"

She shook her head and dropped her gaze to stare at the floor.

"Okay, honey. Let's go then."

"Will Julio be staying with us at the house?" Katie waved in Julio's direction.

Paine stood and shook his head. "Yes, it's his house, honey. Why? Would you rather stay somewhere else? I guess I could get us a hotel room."

Julio protested. "No. If she doesn't want me there, I'll get a room, and you can stay at my place. There's no point in you spending money you can't afford."

Before they could start arguing, Katie spoke up. "He has to stay at the house with us. Who else would help you keep us safe?"

Wow. He doubted the girls had overcome their fear of men so quickly, yet something about Julio spoke to them, and they understood he would keep them safe. Didn't necessarily mean they trusted him, but they trusted Paine, and if Paine thought Julio was an all-right guy, then they would deal with him.

"Thank you, Katie. Now let's all get going. The dogs are probably wondering where we all are."

Julio gave them all a bright smile, but Paine saw the cracking around the edges of it. Yeah, everyone needed to get somewhere they could relax and let go of the weight they all carried. His cousins should have a place they considered home, and he hoped Julio would be willing to let his house become their safe zone.

He herded the girls out to his truck, waved good-bye to Julio, and drove off toward Julio's house. Katie and Betsy stayed silent. Were they overwhelmed by everything? Did they understand they would never see their parents again unless they chose to at some future point? He wanted to ask them, but didn't want to scare them.

"Daddy's in prison, right?" Katie's question broke up the thoughts racing around Paine's head.

"Jail. He don't go to prison until the judge sentences him." He grimaced. "But don't worry. He won't be coming back for a while. They have some crap on him."

"Fighting dogs is illegal, ain't it?"

Paine nodded. "Yep."

"So is letting those men take Betsy and me away and do all those things to us. That's illegal, right?"

Checking behind him, Paine pulled to the side of the road and put the truck in park. He unhooked his seatbelt and angled his body, leaning back against the door. Betsy and Katie looked at him. Scrubbing his hands over his face, he thought for a quick moment. Discussing this stuff wasn't something he was good at. Right then, he wished Julio was with them. The other man would know just the right things to say to these two girls.

"Paine?" Katie's voice made him look up.

Those brown eyes drilled into him, and he realized Katie wasn't broken, not in the same way Betsy was. Katie had become hard and uncaring, except with Betsy and Paine. She'd developed a shell that protected her soul from the destructive world she lived in. There were only two people in the world Katie trusted—him and Betsy. She seemed to be taking Julio at Paine's word that he wouldn't hurt or try anything with them. Paine hoped nothing happened to ruin that fragile and rarely given gift.

"Yes, Katie girl. That was illegal, too. Your daddy ain't a good man. He's going to go to prison for everything."

"Will we have to talk to the police about what he did to us?" Katie pleated the fabric of her pants.

"I guess it would be up to you. If you don't want to talk about it, you wouldn't have to. I'd like you to talk to a therapist, though."

She frowned. "What's a therapist?"

"It's someone you talk to about everything that's gone on and how you feel about it. She'll help you figure out how it'll affect you the rest of your life. In a way, she's like a doctor for the mind." He tapped his finger against his temple. "Tries to make your memories not so vivid, and helps you figure out how to feel better about yourself."

"Do you see a therapist?"

"Not yet, but I have an appointment with one tomorrow. See, I need help, too. I'm not big and strong enough to let everything go. It's bottled up inside me and until I let it out into the open, it'll always control my thoughts and feelings."

Katie looked at Betsy. "I'm not sure Bets can talk to anyone right now, Paine. She don't talk much anymore."

Paine reached over and patted Katie's hand. "I know, but that's okay. She don't have to talk if she don't want to. I'm not going to force you to do anything, Katie. I just want you both to be whole again."

The look she gave him held skepticism, and he laughed.

"Okay, as whole as you can be. Yes, I know it'll take a long time to straighten this shit out, but I think both of you are strong enough not to let Uncle Caesar win. And if we all just wallow in our past, then he does win. I'm not going to give him that power anymore."

Katie studied him, and he met her gaze without flinching. If he could convince her mentally, he would have done it. But she needed to make decisions on her own because it wouldn't work if she didn't want it to.

Finally, she nodded. "I'll go to the therapist. Might work. Might not, but it can't hurt. Betsy can go with me as long as the person we're seeing understands she ain't going to talk probably."

Paine smiled. "That's fine. I'll make sure she knows. Oh, would you prefer a man or woman doctor?"

She shrugged. "Don't matter."

"Right."

Katie didn't like either sex, so trusting one of them would be the difficult part. Paine hoped the person he saw tomorrow would be good for them. He started the truck again and merged back into traffic.

"Let's get home."

At least he hoped it became a home for all of them.

*   *   *

"Is that everything?"

Julio stared in astonishment at the pile of clothes the sales associate rang up. Maryanne's chuckle held pure evil.

"Just wait until those girls are healthy and happy. Your place is going to be full of clothes and shoes. You'll be chasing boys away."

"My place? What makes you think they're going to stay with me?" He pulled out his wallet and handed the lady his credit card.

"Yeah, right. I saw that kiss, Julio, plus I've seen how that young man watches you. He cares about you."

He shook his head. "Doesn't mean anything. I'm the first guy who's treated him like a real person. I haven't asked him for anything. Paine sees me as safe."

"Bullshit."

Julio blinked at Maryanne as she swore with a grin.

"I'm not sure who you're trying to fool, but it's not me. You two haven't done anything yet, have you?" Maryanne gave him the evil eye. "He's not ready for that."

"I think he's more ready than you assume, but no, we haven't. I don't want to take a chance on screwing up the case by sleeping with a witness." Julio signed the receipt and got his card back. "Besides, I want him to be sure he wants me because he's attracted to me, not because he's grateful."

They accepted the bags from the clerk and headed out to his car. After putting everything in the trunk, they climbed into the vehicle and he drove out of the parking lot.

"Paine'll always be grateful to you, Julio. You helped get him out of a bad situation. He's been through enough in his life not to value himself so cheaply. Paine isn't going to pay you back for your caring with his body." She settled back in the seat.

"Not sure about that," he pointed out. "That's what his uncle used him for. You were in the room when he spoke about it. His uncle farmed him and his cousins out to associates to repay favors. Why wouldn't he think he has to repay me by sleeping with me? Even though he's said he wouldn't do it, I have to believe some of his attraction to me will be because he's grateful."

Maryanne pursed her lips and frowned. "I think Paine is smarter than that. He knows the difference between what his uncle did and being grateful to you. He's not going to sleep with you because he thinks he has to. He's going to sleep with you because he *wants* to."

"I can't believe I'm talking to you about this." He blushed.

She poked his arm and chuckled. "Julio, you've tried so hard not to bring your personal life into your work, and I admire that, but you have to understand we want to be your friends as well as your colleagues. We like you. You're passionate about helping the animals and you're smart about how you go about it. I know it's probably really difficult to keep your hands off Paine, but you're doing it in order to ensure his uncle goes to prison for as long as the law will allow."

Julio thought about what she said. He had kept the agents he worked with at arms' length for the most part. A lot of it had to do with moving so often as a child. Some children become very outgoing and instantly make friends at every new place. He was the opposite. He became introverted and solitary, finding friends in the animals he collected, strays needing help or just a little love to get them back on track.

He'd promised himself once he got a home and a solid job, he would push his boundaries a little more. Obviously, he didn't do so well. He had very few friends and only Pedro and Santo could be considered close ones.

Maryanne had a point. He needed to open up a little more at work. Of course, not right at the moment. The Caesar case was huge and he didn't want anything going wrong with it. He'd already skirted the lines by keeping Queenie and letting Paine stay with him. If Emerson had a problem with it, he would talk to Paine and see if the man was willing to move to a hotel until the case was over. Which could be a year from now with as many different felonies as Caesar had committed.

"You're right. I'll try to be better. Maybe I'll throw a party after this case is over," he mumbled.

"I'll bring the beer."

He laughed and parked in front of their headquarters. He followed Maryanne up to where their offices were and knocked on Emerson's door.

"Come in."

"Captain." He strolled in and stood in front of Emerson's desk with his hands behind his back.

"How'd it go?" Emerson peered at him over half-glasses.

"It was worse than we thought. Not sure how the people we sent over there the day of the kennel raid missed Katie Addison, but she's been alone since the day her dad got arrested. Betsy, the younger girl, was brought back by some asshole that had her for over a week. I took them both to the hospital. You should be getting the doctor's report at some point today."

Emerson grimaced. "I've heard some stuff from the teams you left at the house. How do people live like that?"

"It's not like the girls had a choice. Their father's a complete asshole and their mother's an alcoholic. Seems they did the best they could. I hate that we dropped the ball on them." He shoved his hand through his hair, tugging on the ends in frustration.

"So am I, Herendez, but we've got them now and it'll be better for them. Did you leave them at the hospital?"

"No, sir. They're at my house with their cousin, Paine Addison. Turns out the safe house we wanted to put them in is being used by someone else. I chose to put them in my place so I can keep a better eye on them." Julio mentally crossed his fingers, since he wasn't telling the entire truth.

"Hmmm." Emerson's tone said he wasn't completely convinced about Julio's motives. "The doctor okayed them leaving the hospital?"

Julio nodded. "Yes, she said their injuries really just needed time to heal. There weren't any physical ones needing medical attention. I left Smith in charge of gathering evidence at Caesar's house. It was awful, sir. I thought the social worker was going to burst into tears. It's the worst I've seen in a long time."

Emerson growled under his breath and slammed his fist onto his desk. "I don't understand how people can treat their children like that. People who have those kind of genes shouldn't be allowed to procreate."

"I agree, sir." Julio shifted. "I picked some new clothes up for the girls. The things at the house were either rags or filthy. I'm going to run home and drop them off. After that, I'll be back to write up my report."

"Fine. Get out of here." Emerson waved him out of the office.

Julio left the office after letting Maryanne know he'd be back. Climbing into his car, he thought about Paine and the girls. Would they be okay staying at his house? Would the girls get too nervous about having him around? Luckily, there were enough guest bedrooms that Katie and Betsy could each have her own room, though something told Julio that for the foreseeable future, they would be bunking together. Katie wasn't going to let her sister out of her sight until she was reassured nothing would happen to either of them.

At his house, he parked behind Paine's truck and got out. He headed inside and called out as he entered, "Guys, where are you?"

A rush of dogs greeted him, and he fell back against the door as they bumped into his legs. *Hmmm...time to teach them some manners on greeting people.* He brushed them back and told them to sit and stay. All three dogs sat perfectly, but only for a few seconds before they popped up, staring at him like he was the second coming of Christ. It was one of the things he loved about animals. So much unconditional love given and such willingness to forgive. People could take lessons from animals.

He went outside and walked in again. They stood in the same spot he'd left them in, but Samson wiggled wildly, clueing Julio in on the fact the pup was going to break soon.

"All right."

He gestured, and they all came to sniff him. This time it wasn't a mad rush or anything. It was all rather polite. When he got a day off, he'd work some more with them until they reacted that way with everyone.

"Julio, we're in the kitchen," Paine shouted from the back of the house.

"Great. I have some bags in the trunk. Could you help me bring them in?"

Paine padded down the hall in bare feet. Julio smiled and nodded to him. "You're going to need some shoes on, honey. It's a little cold out."

"Right." Paine slipped into a pair of boots by the door. "I told the girls to finish their food and we'd bring the stuff to them."

"Works for me." Julio popped the trunk open and hauled out two of the bags. "I talked to Emerson and he didn't seem too worried about you all staying with me."

Paine's eyes bugged out at the sight of all the bags. "Are those all for the girls?"

"Most of it. I might've picked up a couple pair of jeans and some shirts for you. You didn't have much either." He ducked his head, embarrassed at being caught.

"I don't have the money to pay you back," Paine pointed out.

"I know and it doesn't matter. If you want to pay me back, you can do it a little at a time. I'm not in any hurry, and I know you want to build up some savings as well." Julio whispered a touch over Paine's hand as they walked up to the house. "Trust me. I know you're good for it."

Paine nodded. "You're a good man, Julio Herendez."

"I don't know about that. I just know what's right and wrong. I try to do more right than wrong at the end of the day."

CHAPTER 9

Katie and Betsy sat at the kitchen table, skin pink and hair wet from the shower. They wore two of Julio's robes, which they drowned in. There were two empty plates in front of them, along with two mostly full glasses of milk. Katie tensed when Julio came in, keeping her eyes on him like she wanted to be ready in case he moved too quickly.

"Hello, girls."

He nodded and dropped the bags on the floor near the table. Paine did the same with his, but instead of moving away like Julio did, Paine joined the girls at the table.

"Julio bought you some new clothes."

"What does he want for them?"

Katie's question nearly broke Julio's heart again. Shit, what kind of world did that trio live in where everything had a price?

Paine shook his head. "I'll be paying him back from my paychecks. I told you I work at a shelter with the dogs, remember? So when I get paid, I'll give him some of the money. It won't take long to pay him back."

Julio swore it wouldn't take long at all. He was glad he tucked the receipt in his pocket instead of leaving it in the bags.

"Would you like to take the bags up to your rooms and see what I got? There might be something in there that's more comfortable than my robes." Julio stayed on the opposite of the room, but motioned to the pile.

"We're sharing a room," Katie answered him.

"Makes sense. Strange place with a stranger around, too. I'd want to be near my sister, if I had one." He wasn't going to make a big deal about it. He was sure at some point in the future, Katie and Betsy would want separate rooms. He hoped he'd be around to see that.

They gathered the bags and headed upstairs. Paine paused in the doorway, looking back at Julio.

"Go on up with them. I'm going to grab a sandwich and head back to the office."

"When will you be back tonight?"

He shrugged. "Not sure. Depends on how much paperwork I have, but I'll give you a call on the house phone when I know for sure."

Paine grinned. "Great. I'll have dinner ready when you get home."

"You don't have to do that, Paine. I don't expect you to cook for me or anything." He strolled over to where Paine stood. Cupping Paine's face, he met the man's gaze. "I don't want you to feel like you have to do anything to stay here. I'm opening my house to you and your family without any expectations."

Paine's eyes held happiness and caring. "I know that, but I'm not working anymore today, so I have the time to cook food for all of us."

"Okay." He brushed a quick kiss over Paine's lips. "Get up there and make sure we got stuff the girls like. If there's anything that doesn't fit or they don't want, put it in a pile and I'll take it back."

"Thanks, Julio. I appreciate everything you've done so far for all of us, not just me and the girls, but the dogs as well."

"Everyone needs a chance to thrive."

He stepped back and gestured toward the ceiling. "Get on up there, or I'll be late going back to work and Emerson won't be happy about that."

"See you later."

Paine disappeared down the hall, and Julio made a sandwich for himself. He went outside into the backyard and played fetch with the dogs while he ate. When he finished, he patted each dog before heading to his car.

He'd have to get a cell phone for Paine. He didn't like the idea of Paine being out of reach while traveling to and from work. It wasn't like Paine couldn't handle himself or take care of any problems he encountered. Julio just worried about the younger guy. Silly really, considering all the shit Paine had gone through in his life.

Getting back to his office, he waved to some of the other agents at their desks as he wandered in. He dropped into his chair and booted up his computer. Before the screen even lit up, Emerson poked his head out of his office and pointed at him.

"You…in my office now."

"Uh-oh," Maryanne said under her breath as he walked past her.

"Is something wrong, sir?" He shut the door behind him.

"Not sure. We're pretty sure the judge will sign the dogs over to us tomorrow at the hearing. I need you to go to that."

"Certainly, sir." Julio had planned on going as soon as he found out the date.

"Now, what I need to talk to you about is this. What are we going to do with these dogs once we get them?" Emerson rocked back in his chair, tapping his bottom lip with his pencil. "Sit down and talk to me."

Julio took the chair across from Emerson's desk. He leaned forward, bracing his elbows on his knees. "Sir, I've been doing some research on it, and I have to admit the precedent has been set that usually the dogs are put down as soon as the trial is over."

"Shit."

"Yeah. But in one case, where admittedly there was money for it, the dogs were evaluated on a one-on-one basis. The people who did it discovered most of the dogs had the chance to be rehabilitated. They only ended up putting down one or two, and two were deemed unadoptable, but sent to a sanctuary where they'll live out their lives without humans hurting them again. I'd love to do something like that."

Emerson kept silent for a minute or two, and Julio didn't fidget or demand what his boss thought. Emerson was a good agent. He had the tendency to see the problem from all sides, and wouldn't voice an opinion until he worked it out in his head. Julio didn't know how they could offer the Caesar dogs the same chance. They didn't have access to a fund of money.

"Damn."

Julio snorted silently. Emerson obviously couldn't see any way of fixing the problem.

"What do you think?" Emerson pinned him with a hard stare.

"Once the dogs are ours, go on TV and ask for rescue groups to come and check the dogs out. I think the people working at the shelter can judge which ones can be trusted with a little work, though we should see if one of the animal behaviorists for the Humane Society can go in there and evaluate them. I've been out there and spent time with them. There might be only one dog that should be put down." Julio studied the floor under his boots. "I'd be the first one to tell you, I hate the thought of killing any animal because of what humans have done to it."

Emerson nodded. "It pisses me off."

"Must be why we're doing the job we are." Julio shared a grim smile with his boss. "Unfortunately, there's one male that's been fought too much. He can't be trusted around other dogs, and he's very aggressive toward people. I haven't see him make any progress since Paine and I started working with him."

"So he's marked for death as soon as we get custody?"

Julio nodded.

"Fucking bastard. He couldn't fucking ruin his own fucking life. He has to destroy sixty dogs and three kids. I hope he gets shanked in prison."

He'd never heard his boss sound so vicious, but Julio understood exactly how Emerson felt. There had been several times during the investigation and during the follow-up on the case he'd felt the same way. Violence was never the answer to solving any problem, but he still felt like beating the shit out of Caesar Addison.

"The rest of the dogs?"

"Just need time to learn how to be dogs and to trust people. You'd be amazed at how resilient animals can be, given love, care, and time."

Emerson grunted before straightening. "I'll take what you've said under advisement. We just have to make sure we get the dogs first. After that, we'll worry about what to do with them, though I'm with you and would prefer not having to kill them all."

Julio stood up. "Neither would I, sir. I've already filled out the paperwork. I'll be adopting Stu, Caesar's grand champion, as soon as I'm able."

"Really? I'd have thought he'd be one of the most aggressive dogs in the group."

"No. He's done well with Delilah and Samson. I've been taking them with me when I go to the shelter, getting them used to each other. They've made their own little pack with Delilah as the head dog."

He didn't mention Queenie being a part of the pack either. No one knew she existed, and he'd prefer to keep it that way. He didn't want to risk having her taken away from him. He saved her for Paine.

"Good. Get out of here and write up your report. I want the preliminary version on my desk before you leave tonight."

"Yes, sir."

He returned to his desk. Maryanne came over and sat, giving him a questioning look. "Not getting fired or anything, are you?"

"No. He wanted to know what suggestions I had for the dogs after we get custody of them."

"Put them all down." Maryanne's crisp and immediate reply shocked Julio.

He looked at her. "What do you mean, put them all down?"

"You can't put fighting dogs out into society. Not where they can meet other dogs or even other people. They're too unpredictable and dangerous. It's like having a time bomb, but never knowing when or where it'll go off."

He couldn't believe she would say that. Most people who worked for the Humane Society or any of the animal protective groups loved animals and wouldn't suggest destroying them for such a terrible reason.

"You can't prove that. You don't know how they'll be with other dogs or people. Shouldn't they be given the same rights as people? You don't judge people as guilty until they're given a trial. These dogs deserve that at least."

"Who has the time to work with them? We don't." She waved her hand between them. "All shelters are usually run by volunteers, and those volunteers don't have time to work with the dogs either. It's better for everyone if we just put them down."

Julio clenched his hands tight, anger welling in him. "And should we just put Paine, Katie, and Betsy down as well? They're just as traumatized as those dogs. They've been just as abused and hurt. So we just throw them away and give up on them? How could they possibly function like normal humans?"

Maryanne rolled her eyes and crossed her arms. "Of course not. You don't do that to people."

"So you'd willingly throw away sixty lives because they're 'just' dogs? I've heard people say what's the big deal about dog-fighting? They're just dogs. But if we're supposed to be better than animals, we should ask ourselves why should violence against any creature be okay? Where do we draw that line? And why do we punish those who are innocent in all of this?"

Julio pushed to his feet and paced. "Those dogs didn't think fighting was cool. They didn't understand why they were forced to fight against other dogs when there was no reason for it. Yes, cruelty exists in the animal world, but I've found more senseless violence caused by humans, who should know better than any animal out there."

He turned to see not only Maryanne, but the other agents in the room staring at him. He cleared his throat, realizing he was practically yelling. Julio turned to look at Maryanne.

"I'm not saying some of them aren't damaged beyond being able to repair, but they should be given a second chance. Isn't that what we offer to other people caught up in things they have no control over? The dogs are vulnerable and rely on humans to take care of them. It's wrong to arbitrarily make the decision to end their lives without giving them a chance first."

Glancing around the room again, his cheeks heated and he shrugged. "I'm just saying."

"You're right. I still think we'll discover most of them aren't safe out in public, but we do need to base our decision on each separate dog, not the entire group at once." Maryanne stood and patted his shoulder. "Be as persuasive as that when you talk to the judge tomorrow, and you should be able to save all those dogs. For what? I'm not sure, but it's better than the way they were living before."

Julio dropped into his chair and got his computer working. He opened up a blank report and started filling in the form. Now he'd embarrassed himself in front of all his fellow agents, he just wanted to get his work done and get out of there.

*   *   *

The phone rang when Paine was elbow-deep in the pizza dough. He grimaced at his flour-covered hands. "Katie, can you answer the phone? It's probably Julio."

"Okay."

She skipped over to the phone and picked it up. "Hello?"

Paine kept an ear on her side of the conversation while he spread out the dough over the pan.

"Yes, it's Katie. Paine's making pizza and his hands are all dirty, so he had me answer the phone." A pause. "Yeah, we both found some clothes we could wear. Some were a little too big."

He grunted. Most of the clothes Julio bought were too big for both girls. Yet Paine didn't plan on getting rid of them. Once the girls started eating regularly, they would put weight on and they'd need those clothes.

"Thank you." She shot him a look. "All right. I'll ask him."

Katie rested the phone against her chest. "Julio wants to know if

90

there's anything he can pick up on his way home."

"Hmmm." Paine wrinkled his nose. "Tell him to pick up some Oreos and milk. I think we all need a treat tonight."

Pleasure shone in Katie's eyes, and Betsy made a slight noise. Paine had forgotten how much the girls liked Oreos, plus they hadn't gotten treats like that very often.

"Oreos and milk." A soft laugh came from her. "Maybe you should pick up two packages of cookies. We haven't had anything fun like that in a very long time."

Julio would probably end up buying the store out of the black-and-white cookies, along with several gallons of milk, knowing that both girls and Paine loved them.

"I'll tell him. See you when you get home."

Katie set the phone in the receiver and returned to where she sat at the table with Betsy. He watched them for a moment, seeing what their lives could have been like if they hadn't lived with Caesar Addison and his wife.

The girls were dressed like normal teenage girls. Jeans, T-shirts, and hoodies with sneakers and their hair up in ponytails. Betsy still didn't look like she was in the room with them. Her dull blue eyes never focused on one spot for long. It was like she searched for the exits or the ways to escape. Her long, blonde hair hung limply under the lights in the kitchen and while bruises marred her skin, she was far cleaner now than she was when he'd found her.

Katie's hair was darker blonde, just as long, but shiny instead of dull like Betsy's. She wore her bruises like wounds received in combat, and in a way, Paine guessed, they really were. She fought a war every time Uncle Caesar sold her to someone. A war of attrition not to lose herself in the darkness threatening to take her. It was a war Betsy seemed to have lost. Even Katie's gaze was wary. She seemed to expect to have to dodge a hit or break away from someone grabbing her.

The girls flipped through a magazine, and Katie would point things out to Betsy. Paine didn't know whether Betsy noticed or not.

The dogs gathered around the table, and their calm, loving attitudes eased the tension from the room. Paine continued spreading out the dough and worked on putting the toppings on.

"What do you like on your pizza, Betsy?" he asked as he opened the first package of cheese.

Betsy murmured something to Katie.

"We like pepperoni and mushrooms."

Well, it wasn't Betsy saying it, but at least she said something to Katie.

"One pepperoni and mushroom pizza coming up. I think I might put onions on mine."

"You shouldn't."

"What?" He turned to see Katie smirking at him.

"You shouldn't put onions on your pizza, unless Julio likes them."

Paine frowned as he put the toppings on the girls'. "Why does it matter if Julio likes them or not?"

Katie sighed, and he realized she thought he was being an idiot. "Because he's not going to want to kiss you if you eat onions."

"Ummm..." Paine shifted, unsure how to discuss something like that with Katie. He didn't want to act like his attraction to Julio was wrong or anything, but after all Katie and Betsy had been through, he didn't know what they would think of him and Julio kissing.

"Does it bother you that we might kiss?"

Katie gave him a "get real" look. "No, it doesn't bother us. He's not forcing you to do it. Of course, the men we got didn't like to kiss, did they?"

He shook his head without thinking.

"Right, because Julio is a different kind of guy. I can see that, and I can see you're happier here than you ever were at home." Katie stroked her hand over Betsy's hair. "Paine, it doesn't sound nice, but I really don't care what you do. As long as Bets and I are left alone, you and Julio can fuck like bunnies every chance you get."

He gritted his teeth, wanting to protest Katie's use of that word, but what right did he have to yell at her about it when it was how her parents talked around her?

"You know you can't talk like that once you start back to school," he commented, ignoring the rest of what she said.

"Yeah, though I don't think I'm going back to school anytime soon. I haven't been to school in a year, Paine. I'm too far behind."

"I'm going to get my GED. I don't see why we can't get you and Betsy a tutor to help catch you up to where you need to be." Paine opened the oven and slid the pizza in. Turning, he tucked the towel in his back pocket and leaned against the counter. "Do you think you'd like to try that? I don't want you to miss out on an education because of your father."

"I think we need to talk more about it." Katie's serious look told him he wasn't going to get any sort of answer from her.

He was moving too fast. They had just gotten away from that jail called a home and he was already plotting their future. Katie might seem better adjusted than he thought, but that didn't mean anything. She was acting tough, yet Paine knew all her strength would disappear eventually and she would need someone to hold her. He'd be there for both Katie and Betsy. Plus all the dogs as well.

Another murmur caught his attention, and Katie leaned closer to Betsy. He let the girls talk while he got the second pizza ready. No onions went on, not because Julio might want to kiss him. Paine decided he didn't want any.

Who was he kidding? There weren't any because he *did* want Julio to kiss him. He wanted to get as close to Julio as the man would let him. The last couple of nights he'd fantasized about what it would be like to have Julio fuck him. He wanted to spend the night wrapped in Julio's arms and surround himself with Julio's scent. It made him feel safe.

Going through the refrigerator, Paine made a list of items they were going to have to pick up from the store. He would make sure to check with Katie what kind of foods she and Betsy would like. He pulled out lettuce for a salad.

The dogs shot to their feet and scrambled out of the kitchen toward the front door. He tossed the vegetables on the counter before wiping his hands while wandering down the hallway to say hello to Julio.

Neither girl followed him, which made him happy. Julio shot him a bright grin from where he knelt on the floor, petting the dogs. Paine bent and picked up the two bags on the floor.

"Glad to see you were able to get home early," he commented as he held out his free hand to help Julio stand.

"So am I." Julio continued to move forward, pushing into Paine's arms.

He opened his mouth under Julio's onslaught, letting the man sweep his tongue in. They kissed, tasting and nibbling. Paine lost himself in Julio's mouth, not fighting as Julio embraced him, and issuing a low moan as their groins brushed together.

A giggle broke them apart, causing Paine to glance over his shoulder. No one stood in the doorway, so he hoped Katie hadn't seen them kissing. He looked back at Julio, who chuckled.

"Do you think this is how parents feel? Not having time to kiss without witnesses."

"Don't know. Katie already said she didn't care if we kissed."

"Oh, you were discussing me?" Julio wiggled his eyebrows at him.

Paine blushed. "We were actually talking about onions."

"Really? Can't wait to hear how that conversation happened." Julio stretched slightly. "I'm going upstairs to clean up and change. How long do I have before the pizza's ready?"

"You have twenty minutes. The pizza went in about five minutes ago. I'm cutting up some lettuce for a salad."

He swung around to return to the kitchen, and Julio patted him on the ass. Surprise almost stopped him. It was a possessive touch, but not like Paine was used to, and he wasn't pissed off by it either. He liked believing Julio liked him enough to think of him as his.

"Okay, girls, we have dessert." He held up the bags holding the milk and cookies.

Katie looked up from where she stood, cutting up stuff for salads. "Awesome. I can't wait. Haven't had any kind of dessert for years."

The water came on above them, and Paine tried to keep his mind blank of any images of Julio standing naked in the shower.

"Paine, why would Julio let us stay here? It has to cramp his style to have all of us living with him." She waved her knife around in a vague circle.

"There weren't any safe houses for us to crash at. I don't think Julio has much of a style to cramp. He's kind of a homebody, you know. Rather hang out and watch movies or play with the dogs than go out and drink."

The buzzer rang on the oven and Paine pulled out the first pizza. He checked the other one to make sure it wasn't burning.

"Betsy, can you get the plates out of the cupboard for me?"

Might have been a strange request, but he wanted to see if Betsy would do something he asked. Katie started to reach for the cabinet, but Paine shook his head. Waiting a minute to see if she'd do as he asked wouldn't hurt. Katie quirked her eyebrows at him and he shrugged as Betsy stood and went to the cupboard.

They watched as she took four plates out and set them down. She got out the silverware before making sure the table was set. Betsy sat back in her chair to start looking at the magazine again.

"Thank you, Bets." Paine nodded toward the refrigerator. "Can you grab the dressing, Katie girl?"

Katie did so, and they had everything ready by the time Julio joined them. Julio's still-wet hair was pulled back in a tail at the nape of his neck. It gleamed under the lights. Dressed in a torn T-shirt and faded jeans, Julio looked as relaxed as Paine had ever seen him. They settled down at the table and started eating.

Again, Paine was struck by how homey it all was. Like they were a true family. He smiled as Julio gently teased Katie and tried not to upset Betsy. A little prayer went up from Paine to have the chance to keep this happening more and more often. He wanted to stay a family with Katie and Betsy. If they could convince Julio to join them, all of his dreams would come true.

*   *   *

A knock on his bedroom door woke Julio up later on that night. He peered at the clock and saw it was around one o'clock. Grunting, he pushed up and leaned back against the headboard. He tugged the blankets up, making sure most of his chest and stomach was covered.

"Come in," he called softly.

The door opened a crack, and Paine peered around the edge. "Can I come in?"

Julio nodded and gestured for Paine to come in. The blond man slipped into the room, shutting the door behind him. Julio lifted the edge of his covers, offering, and Paine slid under them, snuggling close to him. He wrapped his arms around Paine, and Paine's warm breath bathed his skin with moist heat.

"How are you doing with all of this?" He stroked his hand over Paine's back.

Paine cuddled closer. "I'm not sure. Disbelief my aunt would abandon her daughters like that, yet I shouldn't have been surprised. I mean, she let her husband sell them to strangers. Why should it be a shock she'd leave them on their own? She ain't never been a good mom. Hell, my mom was better than Aunt Daisy. At least she dumped me with family when she left. She didn't toss me out with the bath water."

The goodness in Paine showed—he could give his mother the benefit of the doubt, even as screwed up as she was. Julio doubted Paine's mother could have known her brother and sister-in-law would have done what they did to Paine.

"Has your mother ever tried getting back in touch with you? Or have you tried finding her?"

Rearing back, Paine looked at him like he was crazy. "Why would I

95

do that? Hell, just because she gave me up don't mean she did it out of the goodness of her heart. I doubt caring about me had anything to do with why she left. All I'm saying is she's better than Aunt Daisy, which ain't saying much."

Okay, the guy had a point. Didn't mean Paine's mother couldn't have gotten her act together since then, though.

"If you could, would you want to see her?"

Paine frowned. "I don't think so. It's not like I feel anything for her. She might be my biological mom, but she don't mean nothing to me. In face, I kinda resent her for leaving me with those two."

"I can understand that." Julio saw Paine's eyelids droop. "Why don't we talk about it tomorrow? Let's get some sleep and see where we are when we wake up."

He eased back, letting Paine flop down on his side away from him. Julio snuggled up close behind him, resting his arm over Paine's waist. He brushed a kiss over the nape of Paine's neck.

"Are you okay with this?" he whispered.

"Sure."

Paine relaxed and, within minutes, was fast asleep. It took Julio a little longer to drift asleep. His racing mind kept him up, trying to figure out what he needed to do tomorrow besides going to court for the dogs.

CHAPTER 10

The tension in Julio's shoulders eased a little after the judge's ruling. The hearing had been a formality anyway. He'd gotten a lot accomplished toward moving forward on the case against Caesar Addison. Hopefully, it wouldn't take long before they actually went to court. No one was going to come and claim the dogs. No one could try it and not end up being investigated for dog-fighting. Julio had made his impassioned plea not to kill the dogs without giving them a chance to be checked out by expert dog behaviorists.

The judge ruled the dogs were the property of the Humane Society, but he decided to order another hearing after doing some research into fighting dogs going back into society. Julio didn't blame the man for being cautious. They could all get into trouble if one of the dogs ended up biting or hurting someone.

He thanked the judge and headed out. Time to go back to his office and call some of those rescue groups. The shelter had been taking good care of the dogs, but their resources were stretched thin. While Paine working there helped, some of the volunteers were still leery about the dogs.

His phone rang as he climbed into his car. After pulling it out, he checked the ID. It was his home number. "Herendez."

"Julio?" Katie's frightened voice came over the phone.

"Yes, Katie. What's wrong?" He started the car and drove out of the parking lot. He managed not to squeal the tires or yell at people to get out of his way.

"Momma's here. Her and Paine are out in the front yard yelling at each other. She wants us back, and Paine won't let her take us."

He could hear the tears in Katie's words.

"Okay. Katie, do you and Betsy want to go back to your mother?" He had to ask.

"Hell, no. She abandoned us to save herself. Plus she let Daddy give us to strangers. I don't know much about being a mother, but I do know you don't do that if you love your children."

"I had to make sure. I'm on my way. Did you call the police yet?"

"Yes. Paine called them when she first showed up, then he went out to talk to her and told me to call you."

God, Paine was putting himself between a crazy drunk and her children. It was almost like standing in the middle of a momma bear and her cubs. It didn't matter that Katie and Betsy didn't want to go back to their mother. Daisy Addison saw those girls as hers, and they were damn well going home with her. Guess it didn't matter to her that there was a warrant out for her arrest either.

"I'm about ten minutes out. Where's Betsy?"

God, this could push the younger girl over the edge. She hadn't really reacted to anything since they brought her to Julio's house, but she had to be happier there than at her garbage dump of a place.

"She's upstairs hiding in a closet. Queenie and Samson are with her. Delilah's here with me. Paine told them to watch us."

Relief rushed through Julio. Nothing would harm those girls if the dogs were there. At one point in their history, pit bulls were known as the "nanny" dog because the breed had the loyalty and uncanny ability to watch their owner's children just like a nanny or babysitter would. While none of his dogs had been taught how to guard, their instinct to protect was strong and would help keep the girls safe.

"Are the police there yet?"

"I hear sirens," Katie announced.

"That means they're coming. I'm about two blocks away. I'm going to hang up now, Katie. I want you to take Delilah and go on upstairs to your sister. Paine or I will come for you when this is all over. Can you do that for me?"

"Yes, sir." She hung up without saying good-bye.

Julio tossed his phone on the passenger seat and almost took the corner on two wheels. As his car skidded to a halt, he spotted Paine standing in his front yard, hands outstretched from his sides, facing a woman who held a pistol in her hands.

Holy shit! Daisy was packing and she'd obviously had a few before she came over, considering the way she weaved in front of Paine. She didn't seem to react to the sound of Julio's car door slamming shut. Before her alcohol-soaked brain realized someone else was there with them, Julio raced across the lawn and tackled her. His hands wrapped around the gun and got it out of her hands without it going off. He thanked God for small miracles.

"Julio, what the hell are you thinking?" Paine jogged toward him. "She could've shot you."

"All the booze has slowed her reaction time. I could've crawled to her and still gotten there before she pulled the trigger." He gagged as he breathed in the stench surrounding Daisy Addison. "Christ, get her away from me."

The uniformed police officers who had arrived right as Julio took Daisy down, dragged her a little way away and handcuffed her.

"You stupid bastard, you couldn't just be happy with what we gave you. You had to ruin it all by ratting out your uncle. After all we did for you, you treat us like this. Steal your cousins away from their mother. Ruin your uncle. I named you right. You've brought us nothing but Paine. I should've drowned you when your mother sold you to us."

Paine froze, and Julio moved to him. He didn't know what Paine would do, but he prepared himself for anything.

"Sold me to you?" Paine took a step in Daisy's direction. "I thought she dumped me on you."

"Hell, no. That whore of a mother knew Caesar was desperate for a son, and we didn't think I could have kids. So when she birthed you, her little bastard, she offered to sell you to us. She needed money for her drug habit and your uncle wanted a son."

Paine reached out for her, but Julio wrapped his arm around the man's waist and tugged him back. He didn't know if Paine wanted to strangle the woman or if he wanted to do something else, but he wasn't taking a chance of Paine hurting her. Not that the woman didn't deserve everything she got.

"A son? Uncle Caesar wanted a son, yet he sold me to men? He beat me and tried to break me down. Why? What was it about me that he didn't like? I'd have done anything for him if he'd shown me a little bit of kindness."

"You were a pussy. Why do you think he called you Butt Boy? He knew you were a fag before you did. He decided to profit from something you'd be doing anyway. Why give away something for free when you can get paid for it? You liked when those men fucked you, Butt Boy. Don't tell me you didn't." Daisy spit in their direction. "When he discovered what a wimp you were, he decided to take advantage of the opportunity."

Julio's stomach roiled and he swallowed hard to keep from throwing up. Where did such hatred and viciousness come from? It wasn't just the alcohol talking. The liquor might have loosened her tongue, but all the poison was already in her brain and heart.

"Fine. I was gay, but that didn't give him the right to whore me out. Nothing gives a person the right to treat another human like that. Nothing." Paine clasped Julio's arm, and Julio winced at the strength in the guy's grip.

"He bought you, Butt Boy. You were his property as much as those damn dogs were. He could do whatever he wanted with you, especially once he realized you weren't going to work out as the heir to his empire."

The police officers looked at Julio. He nodded. "Get her out of here. She's wanted on child abuse and child prostitution charges."

"What? What abuse? What prostitution? I didn't have nothing to do with that. It was all Caesar's idea. I love my baby girls. I wouldn't ever let anything bad happen to them," Daisy protested.

"Bullshit, Aunt Daisy. You sat right there while Uncle Caesar sold Katie to that terrible, old smelly guy the first time. And you turned your back on Betsy when she screamed for you to help her as she was dragged from the house by those meth dealers." Paine growled, and Julio could tell the man wanted to go after his aunt.

"I don't know what you're talking about. Those things never happened. Ask Katie and Betsy. They'll tell you the truth. I'd never let anybody hurt my little girls."

Daisy's sallow skin betrayed how sick the woman was from the alcohol she'd consumed. Julio wouldn't have been surprised if she was on her last leg health-wise.

"You lie, Momma, and the police know that."

"Shit." Paine struggled, and Julio let him go.

The rest of them watched as Paine dashed up the steps to stand next to Katie. He wrapped his arm around her thin shoulders, but didn't say anything. Julio positioned himself between them and Daisy. She might have been restrained, but he wouldn't put it past her to try something, and he wanted to be prepared.

"The police know what you and Daddy did to us, Momma, and

you're going to jail for it. Maybe you can sober up while you're in there because they don't allow liquor in prison." Katie shook, but her voice was strong. Her anger seemed to have overcome any fear she felt about facing her mother again.

Looking at the unsympathetic faces surrounding her, Daisy changed her tactics. Her face contorted into the most hideous snarl Julio had ever seen. It was like she became possessed by a demon. She started screaming, cursing, and spitting at them all. She fought against the officers and almost succeeded in breaking free, but they managed to keep her from hurting herself or anyone else.

"Get her out of here," Julio ordered.

The policemen dragged her to the car and placed her in the backseat, where she continued to rant and rave.

"We'll come in shortly to give our statements," Julio promised. He wanted to talk to Paine and Katie first before he made any other plans.

"Certainly, sir. I'll let the right people know we've got her in custody." One of the officers glanced up to where Paine and his cousin stood. "This is one fucked-up family."

Julio nodded. "It was, but it'll get better now the parents are out of the picture."

"It's sad it has to happen like that sometimes." He gave Julio a small salute. "We'll see you in a little while, sir."

Julio waved and watched the car drive away before turning to head inside. Paine and Katie had abandoned the porch a minute or two before that. Delilah sat by the front door, waiting for him. He reached down and ran his hand over her head.

"Thanks for watching out for them, girl. They're part of our pack now, and we can't let them get hurt. Well, at least not physically. Unfortunately, it's hard to stop the emotional wounds caused by people who should love us."

Delilah woofed softly and, pushing to her feet, led the way upstairs. Julio needed to change out of his grass-stained uniform anyway. He climbed the stairs and went to his room first, changing quickly before going to the girls' room. There he found all three of them huddled in the middle of the queen-sized bed.

Betsy and Katie had their faces buried against Paine's chest. Paine held them close, whispering in their ears. The dogs sat at the side of the bed, watching them with bright eyes. Occasionally, one of them would whine. Julio stepped in and joined the dogs on the floor.

Paine looked up at him. "What happens now?"

"I need you to come with me down to the police station to give a statement. She's already going to be charged with abuse and neglect. We can probably get the prostitution charges to stick without bringing the girls in to testify." Julio scratched Samson's ears as the puppy tried to climb into his lap. "I don't want them having to tell what happened to a jury."

Betsy didn't move, but Katie sat up and faced him. Her eyes were red and her face blotchy from the tears she'd cried. Yet he saw the determination in her gaze.

"I'll go with you and talk to them. We can't leave Betsy by herself, so she'll have to come, but I don't want them asking her questions." Her demands were reasonable.

"I'll talk to them, but I'm pretty sure it'll be okay." He shoved Samson away and stood, brushing the dog hair off his pants. "We should probably head out now. At some point, we're going to have to talk to social services as well."

Paine climbed off the bed. "Why don't you girls get changed and come downstairs? We'll wait for you in the living room."

"Okay." Katie slid off the bed as well.

Julio followed Paine downstairs and waited until they were in the living room before he embraced the younger man.

*   *   *

"Are you okay?" Julio asked Paine.

Paine examined his feelings before he answered. Was he okay? Had finding out his mother had actually sold him changed anything? Why was he not surprised at the news?

"I'm okay for now. No big surprise about my mom, huh? I always thought just 'cause she dumped me didn't mean she didn't love me. Now we know for sure. I wish Katie hadn't heard all that shit her mom said."

"So do I, Paine." Julio ran his hand down Paine's back, soothing him.

"I can't believe Katie's willing to go talk to the police about it. She was going with me to my therapist appointment this afternoon, but maybe I should cancel that. She might not be up to talking about it more than once." He grimaced, hating that his aunt had ruined his day yet again.

"You might have to cancel it anyway. The officer in charge of her case is going to want as much information as possible from Katie about everything. I have a feeling that's going to take quite some time."

Paine exhaled sharply. "Yeah. I'd just gotten myself psyched about going today. Now I have to wait again."

"Your uncle really called you Butt Boy?"

Paine couldn't tell if Julio had been waiting to ask that question, but he could tell Julio wanted the truth. It wasn't that Paine wanted to lie to him. It was just so fucking embarrassing that he wasn't sure he could talk about it.

Julio brushed a kiss over his cheek. "You don't have to talk about it. I really don't need to know."

"Obviously, somehow my uncle figured out I was gay, so he thought that nickname would be hilarious. Used it all the time when he talked to me or any of his associates about me. I never understood why I got ridiculed about getting fucked by guys and the guys who fucked me weren't joked about at all." Paine rubbed his temple against Julio's chin.

"Because you didn't have anyone to defend you. Whereas those guys were big players and had guys willing to kill for them. Your uncle's an ass, but he's not an idiot about self-preservation. He's not going to risk making fun of those guys." Julio hugged him tighter.

"We're ready."

After moving away from each other, they turned to see the girls standing in the opening between the living room and the hallway. They were dressed nicely in khaki pants and long sleeved Henley shirts. Paine winced inside at how skinny they both were. Of course, having a few good meals wasn't going to plump them up any time soon, considering how long they'd gone without proper food.

"We'll have to drive separately since I'll have to get back to my office at some point today." Julio gestured for them to head out. "I'll lock up and call my boss while you all get in Paine's truck."

"Thank you." Katie stopped to meet Julio's gaze.

Julio tilted his head like one of the dogs. "For what?"

"For coming when I called." Katie clasped Betsy's hand in hers. "Not a lot of people have done that for us in our lives. It's nice to find someone who did."

Paine could tell Julio wanted to reach out and touch Katie, but he restrained himself.

"I'll always come when you need me, Katie. I'm here for you girls and Paine, no matter what."

Julio's promise hit Paine low in his gut. No one had ever made that promise to him and meant it. Yet he knew Julio meant every word he spoke. The man didn't make promises lightly. They became like some sacred oath to Julio. It was why the man still watched over Pedro and Santo. Pedro let that little secret slip one night while he and Paine chatted about Julio.

Katie nodded. "It's okay. I know you came to help Paine, but still it was nice to have someone there to keep him from getting hurt."

Julio crouched, a beseeching expression on his face. "Katie and Betsy, I want you to believe this when I say it. Even if Paine wasn't here or isn't around, I'll always protect you from those who would hurt you. My helping you out doesn't have anything to do with Paine, except for the fact that without him, I wouldn't have met you."

Katie still looked skeptical, and Paine knew there wasn't any way to make her believe that. In time, she'd come to realize Julio meant everything he said.

"Let's go, girls."

He waited until the girls were out of the house before he practically tackled Julio. He took Julio's mouth in a determined kiss with tongue and teeth. They kissed until Paine's lungs burned for oxygen. Breaking apart, they panted.

"What was that for?"

"For promising to always be there for Katie and Betsy."

"And you," Julio added.

Paine grinned. "And me."

They headed to the cars where the girls were already sitting in Paine's truck.

"I'll meet you at the police station." Julio hugged Paine before letting him climb in the vehicle with the other two.

"Okay."

He checked to make sure the girls had buckled themselves in before he fastened his seatbelt and started the truck. After pulling out of the driveway, he glanced in the rearview mirror to make sure Julio was behind him like the man said.

"He keeps his promises, doesn't he, Paine?"

Shock rocketed through him, but he tried to act like it wasn't any big deal that Betsy had spoken to him.

"He tries, Bets. I'm sure there'll come a time when he can't keep a promise for whatever reason. But I think I can say it won't be because he doesn't care for us or anything like that. It'll be because circumstances will keep him from it."

Paine wasn't sure if Betsy understood what he meant, but Paine was mature enough to know that no one could keep every promise. Circumstances got in the way and sometimes things happened to stop those vows from being kept. When that happened, he wasn't going to blame Julio. Life wasn't fair and Paine had learned that at an early age.

"Maybe not, but I think he'll try harder than Daddy or Mamma ever did."

Wisdom came from children whose eyes were no longer clouded by innocence. Paine was saddened by that thought. Betsy and Katie shouldn't have to know that about their parents. They shouldn't have been disillusioned by the people who gave them life, until they became adults and realized their parents weren't perfect.

"I think you're right, sweetheart." He reached over and patted Betsy's hand.

His hands shook as he pulled into the parking lot at the police station. He wasn't in trouble, yet Uncle Caesar had put the fear of the police into him at a young age. Paine hadn't gotten over the stupid notion the cops would hurt him if he told about what his uncle and aunt did. Oh, he knew it was all a lie, but it was difficult to break the habits beaten into him.

A knock on the window caused him to jump. He turned to see Julio standing outside with a concerned look on his face. Paine smiled slightly and unhooked his seat belt.

"Come on, girls."

They climbed out, and the four of them headed inside. Paine made sure the girls stayed between him and Julio. He didn't want them freaking out about anything, especially Betsy. Katie just glared at any man who came within five feet of her. Betsy clung to Katie's hand and kept her gaze on the floor.

"Good afternoon, Agent Herendez. What brings you here today?"

Paine glanced around to see a stocky blond man striding toward him. Katie snarled and leapt at the man. Paine barely caught her before she inflicted any kind of damage on the man.

"What the hell?"

Julio placed himself between the girls, Paine, and the officer. "Where's your lieutenant, Iverly?"

"I'm right here. What's the problem?" A tall African-American man stalked into the lobby.

By this time, Betsy had started crying and was huddled at Paine's feet in a fetal crouch. Katie screamed obscenities at the other officer Paine didn't even know she knew. Julio gestured to the officer who had greeted them.

"Iverly's not involved in the Caesar Addison case, is he, Lieutenant Washington?"

The lieutenant shook his head. "No. Why?"

"Because I think we have a problem."

Iverly paled and backed away. Before he got any farther, Julio grabbed his arm, dragging him back.

"Who are these girls? Can't you control them?" Washington glared at Paine, who still held Katie in his arms, trying to keep her contained so she didn't go after Iverly again.

"A woman was brought in about twenty minutes ago by the name of Daisy Addison. She was wanted on charges of child abuse and neglect. She allowed her husband, Caesar Addison, to sell her daughters to men for sex. Something tells me these girls know Iverly, and not in a good way."

"Shit. You can't prove anything." Iverly jerked his arm out of Julio's grip and turned to look at his boss. "Those girls are crazy. Just like the mom. She was screaming at me a few minutes ago."

"I can just imagine what she might have said to you." Julio met Washington's gaze. "You might want to hold Iverly. Don't let him leave until you talk to the girls and Daisy Addison."

"You're going to listen to Herendez? He's not even a real cop. Just one of those animal lovers."

"It doesn't matter what Herendez does. The way those girls are reacting to you makes me suspicious." Washington waved another of the officers over. "Take him to one of the interrogation rooms. Don't let him talk you into allowing him to leave. We're going to get to the bottom of this."

"Yes, sir."

Iverly protested the entire time he was lead away. Paine tugged Katie tighter to his chest, burying his face in her hair and whispering to her. "It's okay. He won't hurt you again. Julio and me won't let him touch you any more. You gotta calm down, Katie girl. Bets needs you."

Julio spoke quietly to Washington, allowing Paine to get Katie to listen to him. He knew the moment she spotted Betsy curled on the floor. Katie tore herself out of his embrace and dropped down next to her sister. The girls wrapped their arms around each other and rocked back and forth.

"Okay, bring them into my office. It might be easier on them to do it there than in one of the other rooms. I'll have a female officer sit with us, but I plan on being there. If Iverly is involved in any way, I need to know about it." Washington frowned as he studied the four of them.

"Could you give us a minute?" Paine hated speaking up. He didn't want to bring any more attention to himself, but he didn't think dragging the girls into the lieutenant's office right away would be good for anyone.

"Certainly. I'll round up the officer, plus I'll have someone go talk to Daisy Addison. See what she has to say about Iverly." Washington marched off, anger evident in every inch of his body.

CHAPTER 11

"What the hell is going on?" Julio whirled to see Paine kneel down and engulf the girls in his arms.

Paine jerked, and Julio took a deep breath. No point in upsetting them more than they all ready were. He had a sick feeling in his stomach about Iverly. Christ, and he had liked the guy, too. Of course, Julio hadn't been close to Iverly. They'd shoot the shit when they met up, but it wasn't like he invited the man over to his house for football or anything like that.

"I'm sorry." He softened his tone and crouched down. "Katie, I need you to look at me. Did your father sell you to Iverly?"

"You won't believe me," she muttered, not raising her eyes from the floor.

"Katie, please look at me."

He kept silent until finally she looked up and met his gaze. He willed her to believe him.

"I will always take whatever you say to me seriously, Katie. No matter how weird or strange or outrageous it may seem. I will never disbelieve you simply because it might not be something I want to hear." He clenched his hands and rested them on his thighs, needing to touch her, but knowing she wasn't in the right frame of mind to let him.

She studied him, seemingly searching every inch of his soul before she nodded. "Yes, both Betsy and me. He was the first for both of us. Paid Daddy a good amount of money to be our first. He wasn't gentle neither. I bled for a while and couldn't move much after he finished. He hurt Betsy even worse. I never thought the bleeding would stop."

Julio held up his hand. "Wait, honey. Don't go spilling everything to me. I only want you to have to say all this once. At least once to the police. What you talk about to your therapist is something different."

"You believe me, don't you? I don't lie, not about stuff like that. He's got no right to treat us like trash and toss us away. It don't matter he's a cop. Still don't give him no right to do that." Rage flared in her eyes, and Julio nodded.

"I believe you, Katie. You have no reason to lie, and I get the feeling your mother's going to say the same thing you do. She's mad and drunk enough to blurt out just about anything. With you corroborating what she says, we should have enough to at least start an investigation on Iverly. "

Julio straightened and held out his hand to Paine. "Let's not keep Lieutenant Washington waiting. Don't worry. We'll stay in the room with you. You won't be left alone with strangers at any time."

Julio took Paine's hand and pulled the man to his feet. Julio let Paine gather the girls and they headed toward Washington's office. Unclenching his fists, Julio breathed deeply and tried to let go of some of his anger. It wouldn't help the girls. They needed him calm and relatively controlled, though knowing he was angry for them might help them get through the next couple of hours. He thought of his boss and stopped just outside the lieutenant's door.

"Go on in and sit. I have to call Emerson again."

"You won't get in trouble for this, will you?" Paine asked softly as he paused in the doorway.

"No. There are other agents working the case as well. This is just as important as the dogs. Trust me. It'll be fine."

Julio wasn't sure if it would be or not, but he wasn't going to tell Paine that. The guy already carried a load of guilt because of the girls. Julio didn't want to add to it. He patted Paine on the shoulder before turning and pulling out his phone.

He dialed and waited for his boss to answer.

"Emerson."

"Hey, Cap, it's Herendez. I might need more time than I thought."

"What the hell happened?" Usually Emerson's bark was worse than his bite, so Julio wasn't too concerned by how upset Emerson sounded.

"Turns out that one of the officers here at the police department was one of Addison's regular customers."

"Fuck. Meth, dogs, or the kids?" Rage swelled in Emerson's voice until he practically shouted the last word.

"Seems that it was the girls, though I wouldn't be overly surprised if Iverly attended a few dog fights as well." Julio shoved his hand through his hair in frustration. "I never saw him at any of the fights, though, because I'm sure he'd have spotted me as well."

Emerson grunted. "Damn the man. Why couldn't he stick with adults?"

"Because there aren't many adult virgins," Julio muttered, sick to his stomach at that thought.

"Okay. Take as long as you need. Just make sure Washington will share the report with us. It won't necessarily help out our case, but I want to stay abreast of everything happening." Emerson hung up.

Julio fought the need to punch something—or someone—but Iverly was already in an interrogation room and Julio didn't want the bastard to get off because of police brutality or some shit like that. He tucked his phone back in his pocket before heading into Washington's office.

The room was crowded with the girls, Paine, Washington, a female officer, and him, but he squeezed behind Katie's chair. He didn't touch her, just stood close so she'd know he was there. She didn't look at him, yet her shoulders relaxed and some of the tension eased from her. He was honored that he had some kind of good effect on her.

Paine sat next to them, holding Betsy on his lap. At her age, she should have been too big to sit on Paine like that, but her growth had been stunted from poor food and neglect. She curled up, her arms wrapped around her waist, and her face turned into Paine's shoulder.

"Okay, let's get started. I'm Lieutenant Jaquim Washington, ladies." Washington met Katie's gaze directly, not ignoring her to talk to Paine or Julio. "I promise I will listen to everything you say with an open mind. I'll have to corroborate it to the best of my ability."

Katie's hands clenched in her lap, and Julio reached out to touch her shoulder lightly.

"It's not that I don't believe you, but these are serious accusations against a highly decorated officer in my department. This will ruin his career. I want to make sure we have all our ducks in a row before we go forward and press charges." Washington nodded toward the female officer. "Officer Aaron here will be taking notes, and we'll be recording this so nothing gets missed."

Paine and Katie nodded.

"Please state your names loud and clear."

"Betsy Addison," Paine spoke for his younger cousin.

"Katie Addison. Betsy ain't gonna talk to you. She probably won't say nothing for a while. That bastard hurt her the worst of the all the guys who screwed her." Katie folded her arms and glared at Washington. "I'll tell the truth and it'll be our truth, not just mine."

Aaron dipped her head, hiding the grimace. Julio smiled, silently cheering Katie on. She was refusing to be a victim anymore, and Julio would support her for as long as she needed him.

"All right, Katie. I can see your sister isn't capable of answering questions right now." Washington softened his voice a little, obviously not wanting to scare Betsy anymore than she already was. "Start from the first time some man paid your father to have sex with you."

Katie narrowed her eyes and appeared to be thinking. Julio shifted an inch or two, so he could see her face. His hip brushed Paine's shoulder, and Paine looked up at him. All Julio really wanted to do was gather all three of the Addison kids into his arms and hold them. They had been badly treated by so many and they deserved so much more for surviving it.

"My first time came when I was twelve, and Betsy's was around that age for her, too. Don't know why. It weren't like there weren't guys around all the time when we was littler, but maybe it was because I grew breasts." Katie shrugged. She glanced over at Paine, who nodded. "Paine had already been getting sold by then."

"Uncle Caesar started using me like that when I was around twelve as well. Katie would've been six at the time." Paine's cheeks flushed, but he held Washington's gaze.

"Where were you when Addison sold Katie the first time?"

Julio stiffened, worried Washington blamed Paine for not helping the girls.

"He'd given me to one of his dog-fighting partners to use as he wanted for two days in exchange for being able to breed one of his bitches to the guy's stud dog."

"It ain't Paine's fault. None of this is. He did the best he could when Daddy let him alone. More times than not, Paine would convince the guy who wanted one of us to take him instead. You got no right to judge him for not being there that first time."

Katie lunged to her feet, hands fisted at her sides. "He got hurt far worse than we ever did. There was a time or two when I didn't think Paine would live to see morning. We won't stay here if you continue to badger him."

The adults stared at her in stunned silence for a moment before

Paine reached out and touched her arm.

"Sit down, Katie girl. It's okay. The lieutenant wasn't blaming me. He's just trying to figure out where everyone was." Paine glanced over at Washington.

The lieutenant nodded. "I wasn't blaming your cousin, Katie. I simply need to know everyone's whereabouts when this happened."

"Well, Paine wasn't even at the house. Mamma was passed out on the couch after she finished a bottle of scotch. Daddy told the guy he could have me for the night if he overlooked something illegal Daddy had done. I didn't want to go. The guy scared me. There wasn't nothing in his eyes. They were cold like a snake's."

"Did your father call the man by name?"

Katie shook her head. "Just called him Officer. All I ever called him was Sir. I might not know his name, but his face is burned into my brain, Lieutenant. The man who raped me the first time was the man who met us when we arrived."

"Sir, I've seen that man around my uncle's house several times over the years. I didn't know he was a police officer or I'd have said something to Agent Herendez. All I knew is that he likes young girls and would pay my uncle money to take Katie or Betsy for a couple of hours. He hit me a couple of times when I tried to stop it from happening. He came to a couple of the dog fights as well, though I hadn't seen him since Julio showed up," Paine added.

Washington scrubbed his hand over his face and swore softly. "This isn't good."

"No, it isn't, Lieutenant. These three should never have suffered like they did. It's not good that the people they should've trusted the most turned their backs on them and abused them in the worse possible way. Are we going to let them get away with it? All three of them can put Iverly at Caesar Addison's house. They've witnessed him committing crimes. It's your job to punish Iverly, especially for what he did to these girls."

Julio's outburst surprised him and everyone else in the room. Washington studied him for a moment before nodding.

"You're right, Agent Herendez. Iverly will be arrested and charged with rape, child molestation, and any other crime this fits under, but I still need Katie and Paine to tell me everything." The lieutenant met Katie's gaze and then Paine's. "I'm not doing this because I want to cause you pain or because I enjoy hearing this. I'm doing this so we can get as much proof as possible."

Katie nodded, and Julio braced himself because the next couple of hours were going to be some of the roughest he'd ever gone through.

*   *   *

Betsy clung to Katie as Paine shut the truck door behind them. He walked around front and rested his head against the driver's side window. Christ, he felt like five miles of bad road on the rainiest day of the year. Holes had been torn in his heart and soul with piles of guilt heaped up on top of the pain.

For over three hours, he'd listened to Katie pour her guts out to Washington and the rest of them. He heard every disgusting thing done to her and Betsy. Paine wanted to go home and take a scalding shower to scrub away all the nastiness left behind. Yet if he felt this way, how must Katie and Betsy feel, having lived it for all those year?

"Don't beat yourself up over all of it."

Julio's hand landed on Paine's shoulder and squeezed. Paine turned to face his friend.

"Why not? I'm sure there were ways I could've kept them from being harmed."

"How? When did you have time to save them? You were dealing with all the same stuff, Paine, and you did your best, but you were so young." Julio stepped closer, ignoring all the people around them. "You should've had someone to turn to, someone to help and protect you."

Paine dropped his gaze to Julio's chest, covered in a dark green T-shirt. He reached out and rested his hand over the spot where Julio's heart beat. The steady pulse soothed him and he swayed.

"Fuck."

Suddenly, Julio engulfed him in a tight embrace. Paine laid his forehead on Julio's shoulder and breathed in the spicy scent he'd come to associate with the man. He bit his lip to keep the tears at bay.

"Is Paine all right?"

Katie's question came from behind him. He stiffened and straightened, worried something might be wrong. After turning, Paine checked her out.

"Are you and Betsy okay?"

Neither girl had shed a tear while Katie recounted their harrowing experiences. Paine figured Betsy was probably still locked away from her feelings. All she had done was huddle close in his arms as Katie spoke. All the anger Katie felt on Paine's behalf had faded away as she spoke, turning into a chilly, robotic voice like she was retelling a movie she'd seen at some point in the past.

"We're fine, Paine." She sighed. "Well, as far as we'll be for a while now. But I think we need to get Betsy home. She feels safer at Julio's place with the dogs."

"Do you think Betsy would like to see the other dogs?" Julio shifted so he could see both of them.

Paine shot Katie a questioning look. Katie glanced over her shoulder to where Betsy sat, practically on the floor under the dashboard.

"There aren't usually a lot of people at the shelter, especially at this time of the day. You could help Paine with the dogs, and maybe seeing them will help Betsy get rid of some of her own pain."

Paine looked at Katie again, and she shrugged.

"It couldn't hurt, and you can always run us home if she can't deal with it."

Her suggestion was a good one, so Paine decided to go with it. The dogs always managed to lift his spirits when he was depressed. Hopefully, they could do the same with Betsy.

"I'll call you when I'm on my way home," Julio promised.

"Good. I'm not sure how much I'll feel like cooking tonight." By the time they all got home that night, Paine figured they would all crash early.

"Don't worry, babe. I'll grab something for us on the way home or I can make something. How do you think I fed myself before you came along?" Julio's smile warmed his heart.

"I just don't want you to think we're gonna sponge off you." He hated not doing something to make up for taking over Julio's house.

Julio laughed. "You're not sponging off me. I offered my house because I want you there. Having Katie and Betsy there doesn't cause any problems. Heck, my house was rather lonely and empty before you all moved in, even with Samson, Delilah, and Queenie."

"Thank God it's a big house. You'll have a fourth dog soon, once they get done evaluating Stu."

"People always asked me why I bought such a big place for just me and two dogs. Maybe, in the back of my mind, I knew my family would expand and I'd need all that room." Julio checked his watch. "Now I have to head out. There's some more paperwork I have to do, but we're getting closer to taking this to court."

"I'll be glad when this is all over." He opened his door and climbed in.

Julio leaned into the window and brushed a quick kiss over his cheek. "So will I. Then we can spend a lot more time together."

"And maybe even get naked together," he whispered, enjoying the blush coloring Julio's face.

"That could be arranged." Julio inched forward a little to see around Paine. "Bye, girls. I'll see you tonight. Have fun at the shelter."

Katie nodded, but Betsy ignored Julio, which they'd all come to expect.

"Be safe." Julio slapped the side of the door as he stepped away.

Paine started the truck and pulled away from the police station. He drove toward the shelter, letting his mind wander over the things he had to do to help the girls. He would call the therapist and make a new appointment for all of them. He hoped Dr. St. Martine would have some suggestions for a specialist in the kind of abuse Katie and Betsy had gone through. The one he was going to see would be fine for him, but the girls' issues went far deeper than his.

He snorted silently. Yeah, he could shovel shit with the best of them. Having sex with a guy might bring his baggage to the surface, but something told him that Julio would be gentle with him and not push him if he wasn't ready. The kissing and touching they'd been doing was good to teach him that sex could be good and not hurt.

Of course, most of the men who fucked him didn't want to kiss him. Paine was just a body to them. Something they could fuck without having to worry about emotions. They used him to get their rocks off.

Julio was different. Yes, it took a while for him to understand Julio didn't want him just for the sex, which Paine figured was going to be the first time he ever made love to anyone. Julio seemed to like him as a person. He didn't look down on Paine because Paine never finished high school or didn't speak proper English sometimes. Julio encouraged Paine to turn his life around, to become something more than what Uncle Caesar always told him he would be. For that respect alone, Paine would have liked Julio.

Yet his feelings were going deeper than just like. Paine worried he was falling in love with Julio, and while he knew Julio cared for him, did the man love him? Would Julio be willing to hitch his wagon to Paine's and have a future together?

Paine glanced over at Katie and Betsy. Katie had coaxed Betsy back up on the seat and they stared out the window together, heads together like they were communicating through their thoughts. Any decision

Paine made would be tied to them from now on. He wasn't going to let the state take them from him. They'd lost so much all ready and didn't need to lose him in the process.

"What are you thinking about?"

He met Katie's gaze and shrugged. "Too many things to really make sense of it all."

She nodded. "We have a problem, don't we?"

"What kind of problem?" Paine hadn't seen or heard anything that would be considered a problem.

"Julio really likes you, but now you've got us to take care of or, at least, you think you need to take care of us. Maybe it's guilt or maybe it's just you know that family takes care of each other." Katie frowned, kneading the fabric covering her thigh. "I don't want to screw things up for you."

Paine shook his head. "Julio and me got things to talk about, Katie, but I guarantee, you and Betsy ain't a problem between us. Julio gets that I won't abandon you. Never again."

Katie didn't seem overly convinced, but Paine let it go. She needed time to accept they would never go back to their parents and never return to that kind of life again. Having been free for only a few days wasn't going to fix a lifetime of issues.

"Here we are."

He pulled into the parking lot of the shelter. There was only one other vehicle there, which was a large truck. Frowning, he stopped Katie and Betsy from getting out of the truck. He dug into his pocket and pulled out the cell phone Julio had gotten him the other day.

Paine scrolled through the numbers until he got to Xavier's number. No one else was supposed to be around that day except Xavier and that wasn't the man's usual ride.

"Hey, Paine, what can I do for you?"

He couldn't help but smile at the friendly greeting, considering how distrustful Xavier had been when he first met Paine.

"Are you at the shelter?"

"No. Why?" Xavier's tone changed to concern.

"Because there's a truck here that I ain't familiar with, and I know you was the only one coming in today. I don't got a good feeling about this, Xavier."

Uneasiness settled into his stomach. There was something about the truck that tickled the back of his mind, like he'd seen it before somewhere. Yet he couldn't decide where he might have glimpsed it.

"Damn," Xavier muttered. "Okay, I'm calling the cops. I want you to get away from there."

"I'll drive down the road a little bit, but I want to be around in case they leave. I can follow them until the cops show up." He thumped his hand against the steering wheel.

"Okay, you get out of there. I've got to talk to the police now."

Xavier hung up, and Paine handed the phone to Katie. Before he could turn the truck on, he saw two men come from around the side of the building. They dragged Stu between them. The big pit struggled and fought as best he could against the catchpoles the men used. Both men bore bites where Stu had gotten them before they managed to subdue him in a way they could move him without being injured more.

CHAPTER 12

"Fuck!"

"Paine, where are those guys taking Stu?" Katie glanced back and forth between him and the men. "I thought Julio was taking Stu as soon as they let him."

Unbuckling his seat belt, Paine made the only decision he could. There wasn't any way he was going to let those men steal Stu. Especially now since he remembered them. They were two men who ran another dog kennel that fought with Uncle Caesar from time to time when they arranged the fights.

"Katie girl, I need you to take the truck and get out of here. Just go down the road to where the gas station is. Turn in there and wait until you see the police go by."

"Paine, you shouldn't try nothing. Wait until the police get here. They take care of things." Katie laid her hand on Paine's arm.

"I can't wait. I don't want anything more to happen to Stu. Look, he's bleeding. They must've kicked him or something. Those guys used to compete against Uncle Caesar, Katie. They want the dogs for fighting, not for any other reason." He looked at her. "Do as I told you. You have to watch over Betsy. I'll be okay. Xavier called the police. I'm sure they'll be here soon."

Katie didn't look happy, but she seemed to realize Paine couldn't be talked out of his course of action. "All right. Go because they just noticed us, and I need to get Betsy out of here."

Paine climbed from the truck, and Katie slid over behind the wheel.

It didn't matter if she knew how to drive or not. Paine just wanted her out of the way in case the men had guns.

"What are you guys doing with Stu?"

Stu lunged toward Paine, but yelped as the men jerked him back. Paine clenched his hands, hating that Stu was hurting, but Paine didn't want to make a move until Katie was out of range. His truck started and he saw the guys' gaze go over his shoulder to where his vehicle was backing out.

"Hey, ain't that Addison's daughter?" One of the men nodded toward the truck.

"Yeah." The bigger of the two glared at Paine. "That would make you Butt Boy, wouldn't it?"

Paine didn't answer.

"So you here to help us get your uncle's dogs? The fucking feds might have arrested Caesar, but we don't plan on letting his best dogs get put down. This stud will father some good pups, plus he'll win us some money in the ring." The first guy, whose name Paine remembered was Squeaky, grinned at him.

"No, dumbass. Don't ya remember what Caesar told us when we met up with him in jail? He said this fag ratted him out to the feds. Not just about the dog-fighting, but about the meth as well. Ruined Caesar and the man's probably going to prison for a long time." Bauer was the other guy's name.

Squeaky nodded. "Right, dude. Caesar told us after he found out where his dogs were being kept. Hey, fag, where did Queenie go?"

Paine didn't move as Squeaky stalked toward him. Of course, by doing that, he left Bauer holding Stu on his own. No matter how strong Bauer was, Stu was angry and that lent strength to the pit's movements. Paine watched that fight for a second before turning his full attention to Squeaky.

"She's at a place where she's safe from assholes like you two. What? You looking to fuck me? Maybe you guys are faggots as well. I've seen how you stare at my ass, Squeaky. Do you want me or maybe you'd rather have Bauer fuck you? Hell, he looks like he enjoys a tight ass wrapped around his cock."

"Shut the hell up, you pussy."

Squeaky dove for him, and Paine dodged out of the way, driving his fist into Squeaky's side as the man flew past him. A high-pitched scream turned his attention away from Squeaky.

Stu hung from Bauer, his jaws clamped around the man's forearm.

Blood dripped from around Stu's teeth, and Bauer howled as he struck the dog over and over with his fist. Paine raced toward them, not wanting Stu to endure any more pain from his tormentors.

"Stu, release," he yelled as he tackled Bauer.

Stu let go and dropped, but instead of running away, Stu stayed. Paine caught glimpses of the black dog while rolling on the ground with Bauer. Losing his focus could be deadly for both him and Stu. When he thought about Squeaky, he wondered why the other man hadn't joined in, but then Bauer head-butted him and stars danced in Paine's vision. Holy shit, a headache was already blooming behind Paine's eyes.

Bauer pinned him to the ground and started punching his head, hard and furious. Paine couldn't stop the blows from landing with his arms stuck under Bauer's knees. Blood covered him and he couldn't tell if it was his or Bauer's.

Where was Stu? Where was Squeaky? God, Paine hoped Squeaky hadn't hurt Stu worse. Paine fought against the blackness threatening to overwhelm him. He couldn't pass out, no matter how beat up he got. Stu and the other dogs counted on him to protect them from the humans who hurt them.

Suddenly, Bauer's weight left him and he lay there, gasping and trying to focus out of his blurry eyes. A stranger came into his line of sight.

"Man, didn't we just see you at the station? You must be having the suckiest day of the year."

Paine blinked and tried to sit up. The speaker pressed a hand to Paine's chest and shook his head.

"You need to stay down until the paramedics get here to check you out."

"What about Stu?" He needed to know the dog was okay.

"Which one's Stu?" The man looked away for a second.

"The dog." Paine breathed and a sharp pain shot through his side like a hot knife through butter. "Fuck!"

"Lie still. The dog's being taken care of."

"Be careful with him. He's hurt pretty bad and he's upset." All Paine could think of was that Stu would strike out in fear and pain, and the judge in charge of his case would decide to put him down because of it.

"We know. Don't worry. The guy who runs the shelter is here and he said to tell you he was calling Julio. Also, there are two girls here who say you're their cousin."

"Shit. Katie and Betsy. I forgot about them. Are they okay?" He rolled his head to the side, squinting to make out the girls standing to the side. "Can they come over here while we wait for the paramedics? Where are Bauer and Squeaky?"

"The guy we pulled off you is being cuffed as we speak. I don't know where the other one is." The guy waved to Katie and Betsy. "You girls come talk to your cousin and keep him calm until we get help here for him."

Katie dropped to her knees next to him and grabbed his hand. Betsy didn't say anything or touch him, but she stayed close. All the noise and men moving about bothered her, Paine could tell, yet she didn't want to be any farther away from him than she was.

"What the fuck was you thinking, Paine?"

He grunted before getting anything out. "Language, Katie. You gotta learn how to talk better and without so much cursing."

She waved away his words. "Whatever. What were you thinking? If Stu wasn't there, you'd have been hurt even worse."

"How is Stu, Katie girl? Is he okay?"

"I don't know. The shelter dude came and managed to get a leash on him. He took him back inside and they said there's a vet on the way to look at him." Katie sighed. "Should I call Julio?"

Paine bit his lip as another shock of pain rocketed through him. "He knows what happened here. Xavier called him since these dogs are part of his case."

"The cops should've had guards on this place," Katie muttered, easing back on her heels and glancing around.

"No one except the agents on the case and the court was supposed to know where the dogs were being kept. Xavier knew, but his volunteers weren't officially told. I guess they figured it out when the news broke, though."

"Okay, Paine, the paramedics are here, and so is Julio," Katie warned him just as they descended on him.

"Do I need to guard you twenty-four/seven, Paine?" Julio dropped down next to Katie, his gorgeous face full of worry and fear.

Paine tried to touch Julio's cheek, but lifting his hand seemed impossible at the moment. Julio grabbed it and smiled slightly.

"I'm sorry," Paine whispered.

"Don't be sorry, babe. I should've known you'd do whatever you thought was right to keep the dogs and the girls safe. I'm sorry you were hurt, but you stuck up for them, Paine. I'm proud of you."

Julio leaned in and kissed his cheek before the paramedics asked them to back up and let them do their work.

"Wait. Julio, can you go and check on Stu? He was beat up pretty good and Xavier called a vet to take a look at him."

"I'll go and do that right now." Julio climbed to his feet and glanced over at the girls. "Betsy, would you like to go with me to check on Stu?"

Something in the stiff way she stood must have alerted Julio to the fact all the people around her overwhelmed her. She nodded and moved closer to Julio, still not touching him.

"Let's go. Katie, can you stay with Paine?"

The older girl nodded and edged to the side, so Paine could still see her, but she was out of the way of the medical guys.

Paine winced as they poked and prodded him. He answered their questions and tried to move what they asked him to. They rolled him onto a board and lifted him onto the gurney. The paramedics were loading him into the ambulance when Julio came back.

"How's Stu?"

Julio grimaced. "He got beat good. A lot of bruising and a broken rib. There's also a few cuts, scrapes, and internal bleeding. The vet thinks he can get all of it taken care of, and the only thing will be Stu having to take time to recover. That's no big deal. He'll be coming home with us as soon as the vet says it's okay. Delilah will keep an eye on him."

"So will the rest of us," Paine promised. "The paramedics say I have to go to the hospital for x-rays."

"He'll probably end up staying the night. He took some good knocks in the head and the doctors will want to make sure he doesn't have a concussion." One of the paramedics looked up from the form he was filling out. "Do you want to ride with him?"

Julio shook his head. "I'd love to, but I have to get the girls taken care of before I come. I don't think Betsy should be spending any more time at the hospital."

Paine nodded. "You're right. Katie girl, will you and Betsy be okay on your own at Julio's? The dogs will be there."

"And I'm going to have Pedro stop by to check on them." Julio looked at Katie. "Don't worry. He won't come in the house or anything. I'll leave his number with you as well. In case you need something and I'm not home yet."

"We've been on our own before," Katie pointed out.

"We know, but you don't have to do that any more. There are people who care for you and we want to make sure you're okay." Julio touched Katie's arm at the elbow. "You don't need to take on all the responsibility, Katie. We're here to help you."

Paine blinked back the tears in his eyes. God, for how long had he wanted to hear someone say that to him? How many nights had he lain on the floor of the main dog kennel, staring up at the ceiling, and hurting in so many places, but mostly his heart? How many nights had he wished for someone, anyone, to take his burden from him?

Now there was a man who would take all Paine's hurt and worries on his own shoulders and carry them as far as Paine needed. This extraordinary man was willing not only to take Paine's, but he would accept Katie and Betsy's pain as well. Paine knew Julio was a special man, and he was all Paine ever wanted from now on.

*   *   *

Julio met Paine's tear-filled eyes and he wondered what the younger man was thinking. Emotion brimmed in Paine's beautiful blue eyes, making Julio's heart skip a beat. Christ, this man could get to him quicker than any other person Julio had ever met.

"We have to go, sir." The paramedic sounded reluctant to interrupt whatever was going on between them.

"Right. I'll go drop the girls off, call Pedro, and come to the hospital. Don't worry about the dogs. Emerson is putting two agents out here to guard them. It looks like Stu was the first one they went for. None of the other dogs are hurt. They're just upset and nervous."

"All right." Paine looked at Katie and Betsy. "You'll be okay. I know you can take care of yourselves, but let Pedro come and look in on you. He's a good guy and a really good friend of Julio's. He won't hurt you."

"Fine. You just better get your butt back to Julio's tomorrow, and no more getting hurt for any of us."

Julio nodded when she glared at him. "Yes, ma'am, I think he's got the message. Come on. Paine needs to get to the doctor's and Betsy needs to get home."

He brushed another butterfly kiss over Paine's bruised cheek. "I'll see you in a little bit."

Stepping back, he watched the paramedics fasten the gurney down and when they nodded, he shut the door and pounded on it. The driver took off, sirens and flashers going. Julio led the way to where he'd left his car, parked crooked and the driver's side car hanging open.

"In a bit of hurry?" Katie shot him an amused glance.

"Can you blame me?" He unlocked the door before remembering Paine's truck. "Shit, how are we going to get Paine's truck home?"

"I can drive it," Katie offered.

Julio shook his head. "You might be able to drive it, but you don't have a license, so we're going to pass on that. We'll lock it up and leave it here. Xavier's going to be here most of the night, along with the two agents. Nothing should happen to it."

They climbed in the car and took off. Julio didn't like the idea of leaving the girls alone at the house, but he also knew that Betsy couldn't take much more. She clung to her sanity by her fingernails, and each minute brought her closer to letting go totally. He grabbed his phone from the center console and punched in Pedro's number. He hit speaker so he could talk while keeping both hands on the wheel.

"Yes?"

"Hey, Pedro, I know Santo's home, but I need to ask a favor. It won't take long and you don't have to open your house to anyone," Julio blurted.

"Julio, what's wrong?" Pedro knew him too well.

"Some guys tried to steal Stu and the other dogs from the shelter. Paine caught them and he got beat up. He's going to the hospital, but I don't want to leave his cousins completely by themselves at my place. Could you stop by and check in on them in an hour or so? Katie's pretty self-sufficient, so it's more to make me feel better than for her."

He shot a quick look over at Katie, who rolled her eyes, but didn't protest. Maybe she realized he was doing this because he cared for her, not because he thought she wasn't capable of taking care of herself and Betsy.

"Sure. Santo has a meeting tonight anyway. Do you want me to bring them some food or something?"

"Katie, are you and Betsy hungry? Would you like Pedro to bring you something to eat or do you want to make it on your own?"

Katie bent a little to whisper to Betsy. A slight nod of the head was all the response she received from the younger girl, but it was enough.

"If he don't mind, he can bring us something. We don't care what. As you probably figured, we ain't picky eaters."

"I heard that. Okay, I'll bring them something in about an hour or so. Do I just leave it on the doorstep or what?"

"Follow their cues, Pedro. If they're willing to have you in the house, they'll let you in. I'm not too concerned about their safety. The dogs are there and they'll make enough noise to alert the neighbors. Also, I talked to Washington, the lieutenant in charge of their case, and he's going to have a patrol car drive past my house every hour. Katie has my cell number and she knows how to dial nine-one-one if needed."

Pedro inhaled sharply. "God, when will the drama end for you?"

Julio's laugh sounded rough around the edges. "I don't know, man. I'm hoping as soon as the bastard is in jail. Anyway, be careful. One of the guys got away, which is why everyone will keep a close eye on the dogs and the girls. We don't want him coming back after any of them."

"Good plan." Pedro sighed. "I'll be over after my last appointment. Are you sure you don't want me to stay with them until you get home?"

"No. I don't think Betsy could handle that. I know you're not going to hurt either of them, but after everything that's happened to them, it'd take more than just my word to make them trust anyone." Julio turned onto his street. "I appreciate you just bringing the girls some food and making sure everything's okay. I'll call them later as well. I won't spend the night at the hospital with Paine. Once he's settled in a room, I'll be home."

He said it both to Pedro and Katie. She nodded and unbuckled her belt before undoing Betsy's. They had pulled into Julio's driveway.

"Probably wise. You don't need to stay with Paine and leave the girls home alone. I guess you'll just have to wait until your boyfriend gets home before you can spoil him," Pedro teased.

"And I plan on it. God, if anyone deserves to be spoiled, it's Paine." Julio climbed out of the car and followed the girls up to the front door. "I'll call you later to let you know how Paine's doing. Tell Santo I said hi."

"I will. You need to come over for dinner some night. Paine and the girls can come as well. If the girls feel up to it," Pedro offered.

Julio let them in, and the dogs greeted them politely without rushing or jumping. He frowned, wondering when that training had happened. He'd planned to do it when he had time, but there wasn't enough time in the day lately.

"It might have to wait for a while, but it sounds like a date." He smiled. "I've got to go. Thanks for doing this, Pedro. I really do appreciate it."

"Hey, man, you've done more for me and Santo. That's what friends do for each other. Tell Paine we're thinking of him." Pedro hung up.

After stuffing his phone away, Julio studied the three dogs sitting in front of him, patiently waiting for scratches. He knelt and starting petting each dog.

"So who taught you some manners, huh?"

"Paine did, along with our help." Katie stood in the hallway, arms wrapped around her waist. Betsy had disappeared upstairs or into the kitchen.

"I knew he was good with dogs. I've been meaning to work with them on some things, but haven't had time lately." He finished the petting and stood. "I'm going to head to the hospital. You've got my number. Call if you need anything, and Pedro will be over in an hour or so."

"We'll be fine. Tell Paine not to bother the nurses too much. He needs to come home." She turned and walked away from him.

"I will."

He locked the door behind him as he left. The dogs had scrambled after Katie when they realized he was leaving again. After getting back into his car, he sat there, resting his forehead on the steering wheel. Exhaustion weighed down his shoulders. When this case was over, he was going to take a vacation and just relax in his backyard or something.

He'd never been so wrung out by a case before. Maybe because he'd never been so emotionally invested in one. The three people he cared about so much were going to break his heart. Sitting back, Julio rubbed his chest and sighed before he started the car. Making sure Paine wasn't hurt worse than he looked was Julio's first priority, then he'd move on to the next problem. That was all he could do right then.

An hour later, Julio sat beside Paine's bed, grinning as Paine pouted.

"It ain't funny." Paine tossed a crumpled up piece of paper at him.

Julio caught it and threw it toward the wastebasket. "It is a little. You're pouting like a little kid who can't get ice cream for dessert. It's just for one night, Paine. I'll be back first thing in the morning to pick you up and take you to the house. The doctors want to make sure you're okay."

"I know. I don't like being away from Katie and Betsy." Paine huffed and looked away. "I know it's probably because I feel guilty about leaving them alone and shit like that. But I'm like their big brother or something. I have to be there to protect them, especially now."

He leaned forward and patted Paine's hand. "I understand, but it's not like they're by themselves. The dogs are with them, and there's a patrol car driving by the house every hour. Pedro called a few minutes ago and said he dropped off food for them and as far as he could see, Katie was doing okay. Betsy didn't come out to greet him, but we knew that wouldn't happen. I'd be surprised if we saw Betsy for a day or two, except to eat."

"Not even then. Katie will take her food to her." Paine fidgeted with the sheets. "I'm glad Stu will be okay."

"Yeah. Xavier said he's doing all right at the moment. He's keeping an eye on him the rest of the night. Looks like Iverly found out where the dogs were staying and got the information to your uncle. Caesar decided if he couldn't use the dogs, then his associates should have them. Bauer's up on assault and various other charges for attacking you and trying to take Stu. The police are still looking for Squeaky."

"That's what happens when no one thinks the cops might be bad."

"True." Julio clasped Paine's hand in his. "How are you feeling?"

Paine eyed him. "Bruised and beat to shit. If I didn't feel that way, I wouldn't be here."

"Smartass. That's not what I meant." Julio scooted his chair closer. "I meant how are you feeling about everything, not physically but emotionally."

Paine's gaze dropped to their entwined hands. "I don't know for sure. I haven't ever thought about how I felt about things. You know? It never mattered before if I liked something or hated it. I just did it or else I'd suffer the consequences. One thing I worry about is that you're going to get fed up with all the shit surrounding me and kick me to the curb."

"I can understand why you'd feel that way, and I'm not sure I can do any one thing to convince you I'll never throw you out or walk away from you because of all this. All I can do is stand by you every step of the way and offer you a hand or shoulder when you need one."

"But why? What's in this for you except a huge headache and more baggage than an airplane cargo hold?" Paine seemed so puzzled.

Julio got up and sat down on the edge of the bed, getting as close to Paine as he could without hurting him. He cradled Paine's black-and-blue face in his hands and smiled.

"*You're* in it for me. Once all the bullshit is behind us, we can be happy and safe. I want you to be more than just my friend, Paine. I want you as my lover, my partner, and my husband."

"They don't allow people like us to marry," Paine pointed out.

Julio chuckled. "I know that, but there's no law stopping us from committing ourselves to each other like that. So we're not legally married…it won't stop me from thinking of you as my husband."

Paine still looked confused. Julio leaned forward and kissed him gently, not wanting to bust open Paine's split lip. Easing back, he met Paine's half-closed eyes.

"I love you, Paine Addison, and I'll keep proving that to you until you believe me. Hopefully, you'll fall in love with me at some point. I'm not going to push you for an answer right now. We'll get through all of this. After the trial, you can figure out exactly what you want to do. The four of us will work on becoming a family because I know you won't come to me without the girls. I'm more than willing to welcome them into my family."

It was a long speech for Julio, but the words tumbled from his mouth like a desperate waterfall of emotion. Paine cupped Julio's cheek in his hand and smiled.

"If I ever figure out what love really is, I'm sure it'll be what I feel for you. I haven't ever felt it or had it returned before, so I'm new at it. I care so much for you, Julio. Please, be patient."

"I'll wait as long as it takes for us to have our happily ever after."

Their lips came together in a quiet promise of love, patience, and caring. Neither of them wanted to rush the best thing they'd ever had. They had all the time in the world and getting there would be half the fun.

CHAPTER 13

"We, the jury, find the defendant…guilty."

Julio's shoulders slumped forward and he took a deep breath. Daisy Addison's trial was the last one they had to go through. It had been a long six months for all of them, but finally justice had been served.

Daisy was going to jail for abusing and neglecting her daughters. Caesar Addison had already been found guilty of dog-fighting, animal abuse, and child abuse among several other charges. The judge in his case handed down the toughest sentences he could, and Caesar wouldn't see the outside of a prison for at least twenty years. It could be more since he was only up for parole in twenty years.

Paine's aunt was facing fifteen years or more, depending on what the judge wished to do. Daisy stood, crying loudly as the verdict was read. Julio couldn't find any sympathy for the woman. What she allowed her children to go through deserved life in prison as far as he was concerned.

"Court adjourned."

Julio turned and swept Paine into his arms. He hugged him tight and managed to smile through his tears at Katie. Betsy had stayed home with Santo. Who would have known the most traumatized of all the victims in Julio's case would become attached to the most damaged of Julio's friends? Of course, in a way, it made sense. They understood each other without ever having to say a word.

Santo accepted Betsy's silence and they seemed to communicate without words. Pedro didn't seem all that shocked by the development, but he knew his life partner better than anyone else. Yet he admitted to Julio one night even he didn't know everything that had driven Santo to numbing his life with heroin. What flaws marked the man in some way other mutilated souls recognized? Julio never brought himself to ask Santo.

Holding out his arm, Julio hid his surprise when Katie joined them in their hug. She had slowly been warming up to him and letting him touch her arm or shoulder without tensing. Maybe Katie had finally come to realize Paine and Julio weren't leaving her.

"Agent Herendez? Mr. Addison?"

They broke apart and turned to see Maria, the social worker, standing in the aisle. Katie stayed between them as they moved out to greet her.

"Hello, Maria. How can I help you?"

She smiled softly at Katie. "How are you today, Katie?"

"I'm doing great, now that my parents are going to prison." Katie crossed her arms over her chest and frowned at Maria.

"And where is Betsy?" Maria looked around. "I thought she might've wanted to be here to see this."

"She's at home with a friend of mine. The only one she really has anything to do with. We all talked it over, and Betsy decided she didn't want to see any of this. She's written her parents off." Julio gestured to Paine, Katie and himself. "We're her family now."

Maria nodded. "Well, that's what I need to talk to you about. We haven't done anything officially about the girls because we understood what they've gone through and how upsetting this all must've been for them. We didn't want to disrupt their lives any more than necessary."

Katie coughed loudly, and Julio hid his smile. He motioned toward the door of the courtroom.

"Why don't we go out in the lobby and talk? I'm sure they'd like the court emptied."

Maria led the way and they found an out-of-the-way spot to talk. Maria grimaced as Paine shot her a worried look.

"Don't worry. It's more of a formality than anything. We just need to make sure your household is the right one for the girls to grow up in."

"You've got to be kidding me?" Katie looked insulted.

"Katie," Paine warned.

"No." She shook her head before whirling on Maria. "How dare you come in and say Paine and Julio aren't the right people to take care of me and Betsy. Where do you get off saying that shit?"

"Katie, Maria didn't say you couldn't live with us. She just needs to make sure."

"No one ever came out to my parents' house when I called for help. None of you cared when Betsy and me were raped or when Paine had to let guys fuck him 'cause my daddy is a complete bastard." Katie waved her finger in Maria's face. "You got no right to say Paine don't care for us. You don't know my cousin or the man he loves. If you take me away from them, I'll run away, and you won't ever be able to find me."

Julio nudged Paine and nodded toward Katie. The man wrapped his arms around the furious girl and dragged her away. After she left, Julio turned back to Maria.

"I'm sorry about that."

"It's understandable, Agent Herendez. You and her cousin are the only stable home she's ever had. However, we have to make a recommendation to the judge. We have to tell him whether we think Katie and Betsy should be placed in the foster system or whether leaving them with you is in their best interest."

"Paine is the best guardian those girls could have. He's got a full-time job at the animal shelter while working to get his GED. He plans to go to college and become a vet tech."

Maria smiled at Julio's deluge of information. "It's good to hear Mr. Addison is a responsible adult, but so are a lot of other people in the foster care system. What I need to know is why he's the right person for the girls."

Julio looked over to where Paine and Katie sat watching him. One pair of blue eyes held love for him and he never wanted to go a day without looking into them. Katie's brown eyes met his with strength and determination shining in them. Katie would do what she said if social services took her and Betsy away.

The oldest Addison girl had dropped some of her walls and let him inside her exclusive group of people she trusted. Julio didn't plan to take that for granted and he'd never do anything to break the fragile ties they were establishing.

Julio, Paine, and the girls were becoming a family, little by little. Each day, Katie and Betsy blossomed into the beautiful young ladies they should have been if their parents hadn't been such fuck-ups.

"Paine's the right person to be given custody of Katie and Betsy. He knows what they've gone through. He went through the same thing they did. All of it. Paine helps them when they have nightmares. He gives up so much of his time for them. Some of it's guilt because he still feels he could've stopped it from happening. He set up counseling for all of them and it's helped."

Maria pulled out her notebook. "I'm going to need to get the name of the therapist they're seeing. I don't ask any really personal questions, but I do need to ask him/her how she feels about them being with you."

"Will it matter that Paine and I are dating?"

God, he hoped not. He didn't want to give the man up, but if it came down to whether or not the girls stayed with Paine, Julio would leave. Paine, Katie and Betsy could keep the house. He'd find somewhere else to live.

"I don't think so. I'll have to look into it, but I don't think the state has any laws against a gay couple becoming foster parents. It's a bonus that Paine is related to the girls. Also, Katie's old enough to make her own decision and I'm pretty sure if we asked Betsy who she wanted to live with, she'd say you guys." Maria shrugged. "I still need to talk to both of them, but it can wait until tomorrow."

"Okay." Julio took her card and tucked it in his pants pocket. "I'll have Paine call you tomorrow and you can set up a time for him to bring the girls to see you."

"Thank you."

He stood and watched Maria say good-bye to Katie and Paine. The duo approached him after the social worker left. He gave them a small smile.

"It'll be okay. We'll do what we have to do to keep being a family, though there won't be any running away at any time." He stared pointedly at Katie.

Katie wrinkled her nose at him, but didn't promise either way. The girl would do whatever she had to do, and if that meant running away, she'd do it.

"Let's go home and let Betsy know. Plus I know Santo needed to be home early because it's Pedro's birthday today." He waved his hand toward the door.

"Should we pick up a gift for him?" Paine asked as they made their way to Julio's car.

"No. I gave Santo some money and he should've taken Betsy out to get something from us for Pedro. Makes her feel useful and she's doing it with someone she trusts."

Julio waited until everyone was belted in before he started the car and pulled out of the parking lot. He headed back to their house.

"Maria wants you to call her tomorrow and set up a time for you to meet and talk with her," he informed Paine.

"All of us?" Katie sounded wary.

"The three of you." Julio watched the street.

Paine gripped Julio's thigh. "Why? Did I do something wrong?"

"Why now? We've been with you for over six months. Why didn't they do all of this when they first took us? I don't understand," Katie questioned.

Julio shrugged. "I don't know. Maybe they figured it would be okay at that time because Paine was a relative, and you needed to get through the trial. They didn't want to upset you any more than you already were. Now that the trial's over, they need to get the paperwork in order. Maria didn't seem to act like there'll be a problem."

"What will we do?" Panic tainted Paine's voice.

Julio covered Paine's hand and squeezed. "Try not to panic, babe. Wait until the recommendation is made. Once it's done, we'll figure out what we're going to do, even if they want to place the girls with someone else. If that happens, we'll talk to Maria and see what we have to do to get them back with us."

Katie leaned forward and poked Julio's shoulder. "I know you'll try."

"I promise. Oh, and Maria needs to talk to your therapists. I guess she needs both of your therapists since you don't go to the same one."

"I can give her the names." Paine twined his fingers through Julio's. "You're right, Julio. No point in buying trouble, especially since we had a good day today. Aunt Daisy's going to prison along with Uncle Caesar. Stu's coming home to stay, and the other dogs are finding rescue homes to be fostered in. All in all, it's been a great day."

Hearing such an up-beat comment from Paine brought a smile to Julio's face. It was a great day and it didn't matter about tomorrow. They would deal with whatever came then.

They pulled into Julio's driveway and headed inside. Following the sounds of singing, they went through the kitchen to the back yard. Julio stopped in the doorway, and the other two paused with him.

Betsy, Santo, and the dogs sat in the middle of the yard. Betsy had three of the dogs sprawled around her. Queenie rested her head on Santo's lap while the man sang. His voice was low and rough, but melodic. He sang in Spanish, but it didn't matter that Betsy couldn't understand him. Her eyes were closed while she swayed in time with the guitar Santo played. When the song ended, Julio clapped and the dogs jumped to their feet. Katie and Paine greeted the dogs, while Julio waded through them to Santo.

"You going to sing that song to Pedro tonight?"

Santo grinned, his crooked teeth making his smile seem brighter somehow. "No, *hermano*, the song I'll be singing isn't appropriate for children or dogs. How did court go?"

Julio rolled his eyes. He knew exactly what kind of song Santo would be singing later that night. After turning, he gestured for Betsy to come closer to him. Katie and Paine joined them.

"Daisy was found guilty on all twenty charges. The sentencing phase of the trial will take place next week, but I think she'll be going to prison for a long time. Now we just have to work out with social services where the girls are staying."

Fear blossomed in Betsy's eyes and she grabbed hold of Katie's arm. Katie encircled Betsy's shoulder with a soft murmur.

"Don't worry. It's merely a formality. Paine, Katie and Betsy have to go and talk to Maria, the caseworker. She has questions she needs to ask, but there won't be a problem." Julio slipped his arm around Paine's waist and pulled the man closer to him. "Betsy, we'll remain a family, no matter what we have to do to make it that way."

*   *   *

Paine met Julio's gaze and smiled. He'd come to trust Julio when the man promised things because he knew Julio would do whatever he had to do to set things right.

"That's good news. You know Pedro and me will come testify on your behalf if you need us, *hermano*," Santo offered.

"Thanks." Julio offered his hand to Santo. "I'll let you know, but you need to get out of here now. There's a birthday boy waiting for you at home. Bets, did you get a present from all of us for Pedro?"

"Yes." She nodded.

One of the major developments, aside from Betsy trusting Santo from the moment she met him, was the fact she was beginning to talk to them more. She spent more time with them every day instead of hiding in her bedroom. Talking to the therapist helped all of them slowly work through their issues.

Soon they were going to have to see about getting tutors for the girls. Hopefully, they could find someone who was perfect for them.

Paine didn't think Katie would ever go back to school, but that would be okay. She could study and try for her GED when the time came. Betsy would probably have to return to school, but Paine wanted to make sure she was ready for it before they sent her into such an environment.

All of that would be worked out later. Right now, they would celebrate being free of Uncle Caesar and Aunt Daisy. A wet nose nudged his hand and he stared down at Stu. The black pit bull sat at his feet, his happy doggy smile belying the terrible beginning of his life. Poor thing was a mass of scars along his chest and sides. Yet the unconditional love he gave all of them was a testament to how a soul can survive if given a chance.

"Why don't you show Santo out, Bets, while we figure out what to make for dinner?" Paine suggested as the group made their way inside.

"Okay."

Santo hugged him and Julio. The man whispered something in Julio's ear that made Julio blush. What could Santo have said to get that reaction from Julio? Paine decided to ask Julio later.

"So what should we have to celebrate?" He opened the refrigerator and studied its contents.

"Can we have spaghetti?" Katie asked, reaching around him for the orange juice.

"Sure. Julio, can you get the pasta out of the pantry?" He grabbed the lettuce and tomatoes for salad.

After Betsy returned, the four of them pitched in to make dinner. They sat down and continued to chat, talking about everything except the verdict handed down that day. By the time the dishes were done and the kitchen cleaned up, it was dark outside, but they still wandered out to the patio. Julio sat on the wide swing they'd bought a week or two ago. Paine joined him, while the girls went out on the lawn to play with the dogs.

Julio wrapped his arm around Paine's shoulder, tugging him close. Paine snuggled into Julio's warmth, breathing the man's male scent in deep. He rested his hand on Julio's thigh and stroked along the inner seam of Julio's pants, watching the girls.

"Do you think we can do it?" The question slipped from his mouth without his meaning to say anything.

"Yes, I do. What Katie and Betsy need more than anything are people who love them. You're their cousin and have proven you'll take any punishment to keep them from getting hurt. Since they've come to live here, I've fallen in love with them and I'd give my life for them and you."

Paine eased back slightly to look up at Julio. "I know. I'm just scared something will happen and they'll take Katie and Betsy away from us. I'm not sure Betsy would recover from that, and we both know Katie would run away before she let anyone place her in a foster home."

Their lips met and a gentle kiss passed between them. He wouldn't let it go as far as some of their kisses had gone. Of course, those kisses were in the dark privacy of Julio's room after the girls had gone to bed. He didn't want to freak them out by too much public displays of affection.

"Come on, you two. If you're going to keep doing that, you need to take your celebration upstairs."

Paine broke away from Julio, his face burning with lust and embarrassment. Katie stood in front of them, her arms folded, but a grin on her face. She motioned to where Betsy had disappeared inside along with the dogs. "We're going to clean up and get ready for bed."

"Do you want to talk about what happened today?" Julio asked, helping Paine stand before climbing to his own feet.

"Nope. We can talk about it tomorrow after our therapy session. Maybe I'll have my feelings worked out by then."

"Okay. Get on to bed. Don't stay up too late." Paine hugged her and beamed with pride as she hugged Julio quickly.

Paine shut the back door, while Julio went through the house, making sure all the windows and doors were locked. He waited at the foot of the stairs while Julio set the alarm. They wandered up the stairs arm-in-arm. They stopped by the girls' room and knocked on the door.

Betsy opened it, and Paine spotted Stu and Queenie lying on her bed. Delilah and Samson had claimed their spots on Katie's bed.

"Just wanted to say good-night. If you need us, you know you can come and wake us up."

She nodded and shut the door before he could say anything else. Julio took his hand and dragged him down the hall to their room. Paine had started sharing Julio's bed when he came home from the hospital and he'd come to love waking up to Julio's warm, solid body.

He laughed as Julio pulled him into the room and pushed him up against the closed door. Julio took his mouth like he was starving for another deeper taste of him. Paine opened, allowing Julio to sweep his tongue and tease every spot that made him shiver.

Paine slid his hands around Julio's back and down to grab his ass. Julio smoothed along Paine's sides, his hands ending up on Paine's hips. Julio leaned into him, their bodies touching from chest to knee.

They feasted on each other until Paine's lungs burned for oxygen. He broke off, let his head drop back, and panted until he caught his breath. Meeting Julio's gaze, he grinned.

"Are we going to have sex now?"

Julio paused and stepped back, keeping contact with Paine, but giving him space. "If you want to. I don't want you to think you have to do it now, just because the case is over with or anything like that. We'll do it whenever you feel ready."

Chuckling, Paine grabbed Julio's hips and rubbed their groins together. He moaned as their erections met. Julio's pants-covered hard length fit perfectly alongside his, and they rocked in harmony for a few seconds.

"Stop. We keep this up, I'll come in my pants and I don't want that to happen. I want to be inside you the first time I come with you." Julio hesitated before going on. "Unless you want to do me."

Shock rocketed through Paine and he froze. Fucking Julio had never crossed Paine's mind. "Really?"

Julio shrugged. "I like it either way. Have you ever topped before?"

Paine's eyebrows shot up and he laughed harshly. "What do you think?"

"I'm sorry. I didn't know if you ever had an experience outside of what your uncle made you do." Julio stepped back, took Paine's hand, and walked backward toward the bed.

Paine grunted as Julio sat and yanked him down onto his lap. He straddled his soon-to-be lover's thighs, enjoying the feel of Julio's cock under his ass. He wiggled and shifted until Julio gripped his hips to stop him.

"You're not helping," Julio pointed out.

"I'm not really trying to," Paine admitted. He sighed and stopped. "Do you think it was safe for any man to admit he liked fucking guys? It's one thing for them to fuck me. I was just a body, not even a real person, just another something for them to control and have power over. But for a guy to admit he was gay, he'd have his ass beat or he'd be killed. They don't accept anyone different. Hell, the only reason my uncle and his associates allowed blacks and Mexicans in was because they had money."

"Makes sense."

Paine laid his hands on Julio's shoulders and stared into Julio's dark, honest eyes. "Would you let me fuck you?"

"No."

His heart dropped, but Julio smiled.

"I'll let you make love to me though." Julio nuzzled his cheek against Paine's hand. "That's what we'll be doing from now on, every time we come together like this. I love you, Paine, and I trust you. You're not going to hurt me and I want you to see someone can enjoy having sex."

Tears welled in his eyes. No person, besides his cousins, had ever trusted him not to hurt them. Julio had treated him with respect ever since they'd first met, and Paine wanted to show how much he loved Julio as well.

He climbed off Julio's lap and lifted the hem of his T-shirt. Before he finished, Julio was there, helping him strip. Again, none of the other men who fucked him had ever helped him undress. They usually didn't even wait for him to get naked. They'd just yank his jeans down, push him onto the bed, and start fucking him.

With each soft caress of Julio's fingers over his skin, Paine realized this was going to be totally different from all the other encounters he'd had. He reached out to start unbuttoning Julio's shirt, but Julio brushed his hands away.

"Let me do you first. Then we'll worry about my clothes."

"Okay." Like he was going to argue with that.

He sucked in his stomach as Julio undid and unzipped his jeans, kneeling as he pushed the fabric down to Paine's knees. Paine braced his hands on Julio's shoulders and lifted one foot at a time for Julio to pull off the denim. He swallowed his laughter as Julio tossed the jeans over his shoulder, obviously not caring where the pants landed.

His laugh morphed into a groan as Julio brushed his lips over the head of Paine's cock. *Christ!* He'd never had anyone touch or suck him there. Very rarely had he ever come from being fucked by the men his uncle sold him to. The only way he knew what an orgasm felt like was by jerking himself off once in a while.

Julio sucked just the crown of Paine's shaft into his mouth and flicked the spongy glans with his tongue. Paine's eyes rolled back in his head and his knees trembled.

"I think I need to lie down."

Laughter caused Julio's body to shake, but the man allowed Paine to slide from his mouth before standing and leading Paine to the bed.

Julio pulled back the blankets and lay on his back.

"Come and straddle my chest."

Paine climbed onto the bed, his knees nestling into Julio's armpits, and he clasped the headboard with a white-knuckled hand. He positioned his cock at Julio's lips with a soft whimper.

Tiny little licks teased his slit and along the entire length of his prick. Julio's hands squeezed Paine's ass, encouraging him to move. He slowly stroked in and out of Julio's hot, moist mouth. Nothing in his life had ever prepared him to experience something like that.

"Julio," he croaked, tingles chasing down his spine and over his skin.

"Do you want to get me ready for you?" Julio asked after letting Paine pull from his mouth.

"I'm not sure I can," Paine admitted, thinking he might explode if he touched Julio.

"It's okay. Roll over. I need to get the stuff."

Paine flopped to the side, landing on his back. His chest heaved as he panted and he swore his heartbeat shuddered his body. He couldn't stop touching himself. He fisted his cock and pumped, savoring the slick feel of Julio's spit mixing with his own pre-cum.

"Got them." Julio swung back, holding a strip of condoms and a tube of lube in his hand. "Did any of the bastards stretch you before they took you?"

Shaking his head, Paine wet his lips and cleared his throat before he could talk. "No. They were more interested in getting their rocks off than with whether they hurt me or not."

"Do you want to watch me?"

"God, I don't know if I'd last watching you finger fuck yourself. I'm ready to shoot right now."

Julio eyed Paine's hard cock swaying slightly with the strength of the pulse pounding in the underside vein running his length. "All right. Why don't you get the rubber on? I won't take long."

Paine held out his hand for the foil packets. Somehow, he managed to tear one of them open and roll the condom down over his flesh. Julio's low moan caught his attention. Glancing up, he saw Julio's head thrown back and one of Julio's hands reaching behind him. Julio's hips started rocking as Julio stretched his own hole, lubing it and relaxing the ring of muscles.

Julio's prick stood proudly from the nest of the black curls at his groin. The younger man couldn't stop himself from wrapping his fingers around the thick piece of flesh, giving Julio a warm tunnel to thrust into. Jerking a guy off wasn't anything new to Paine, but knowing it was Julio he was holding changed everything about the act.

"Paine…" Julio grunted and froze. "I don't want to come until you're inside me. Slick yourself up and we'll do this."

As Paine reached for the lube, Julio rolled onto his back. He hooked his hands behind his knees and pulled his legs up and wide. Paine settled between Julio's thighs and positioned the head of his cock at Julio's slick, stretched opening.

Taking a deep breath, he looked up and met Julio's gaze. Love shone in his lover's dark eyes along with trust. Emotions Paine had never felt before while having sex welled in him. It wasn't just sex. The minute he sank into Julio, it would be making love and there wasn't any going back from that.

"Are you okay, honey?"

Paine blinked and smiled at Julio's concerned question. "Yeah, I'm fine. Just a little freaked out. It's the first time I've ever done this. I'm afraid I'll hurt you or something."

"I'm not about to ask you if it hurt when guys fucked you. I know it did, but I promise, Paine, it'll only hurt me for a few seconds, then it's all pleasure, and you'll blow my mind."

Come on, jackass. It isn't that hard, and Julio'll let you know if you hurt him.

Paine closed his eyes, took another deep breath and pressed forward. As Julio relaxed, slipping into him became easy until Paine was buried balls deep. They both sighed when Paine leaned over and brushed a kiss over Julio's lips.

"Are you okay?" He couldn't help but ask.

"I'm fine. I'd be much better if you actually moved." Julio gave him a slight smile.

"Oh, right."

Bracing his hands on either side of Julio's head, Paine eased out until only the head of his cock rested inside Julio.

"Fast and hard or slow and gentle?"

"I want *you* to make love to me however you want to, though I tend to prefer it hard and fast."

"I can do that."

He plunged back in, and Julio flung his arm over his face to muffle his shout. Paine moved, speeding up as he realized Julio really did enjoy what Paine was doing to him. He loved how tight and hot Julio's channel was. In some weird way, he understood why the men who fucked him would do that, though not why they would do it to a person who didn't want them.

Julio moved with him, moaning and grunting each time Paine nailed his gland. He clenched his inner muscles and drove Paine crazy with each stroke out.

"Oh, God, Julio, this is incredible. Thank you." Panting, Paine sped up, slamming deep into Julio. Something in Julio's face caught Paine's attention. "Touch yourself, love. I want you to come on my cock."

Paine almost came as Julio wrapped his free hand around his cock and started pumping in time with Paine's movements. Only a few more well-timed thrusts and Julio came, spilling his cum all over his hand and stomach.

Throwing his head back, Paine continued to ride Julio through the man's climax until, with one last clench, Julio brought Paine over the edge. For the first time in his life, Paine came while having sex with someone else and it blew his mind.

As he filled the rubber, he stared down into Julio's eyes and saw all his love reflecting back at him. Julio loved him and showed him how much every day they'd been together since that fateful night. Paine learned what love really was with each promise Julio made and kept.

Tears dripped from his chin onto Julio's cheeks, mingling with Julio's. Paine collapsed onto his lover, trembling and crying like he never had before. He no longer had to be strong. Julio would be by his side to support him and encourage him. Paine wouldn't have to suffer in silence anymore. Now he had someone who would fight for him and be his voice when he needed one.

No matter what happened in their lives, their hearts were entwined together forever.

T. A. CHASE

T. A. Chase lives a life without boundaries. Being fascinated by life and how different we all are, he writes about the things that make us unique. He finds beauty in all kinds of love and enjoys sharing those insights. He lives in the Midwest with his partner of twelve years. When he isn't writing, he's watching movies, reading and living life to the fullest.

*   *   *

**Don't miss *Shades Of Dreams*
by T. A. Chase,
available at AmberAllure.com!**

Stephan Colby is on top of the world. He's the lead singer of one of the hottest new rock bands, and his best friend is in the band to share the success as well. In addition, Stephan's madly in love. Yet Fate has a cruel way of kicking a man in the teeth, and when Stephan's world crashes down around him, he turns to his Rock, his bandmate, the one man who has always been there for him.

Rocky Sanicily has always had Stephan's back, and they've been through a lot together. Rocky has also been in love with Stephan for many years, but has never found the courage to admit it. When Stephan suddenly loses the most important thing in his life, however, Rocky must do everything in his power to keep Stephan from giving up. If he succeeds, will he be able to finally tell Stephan how he feels? And if so, will it bring the friends closer together, or tear apart their relationship forever?

AMBER QUILL PRESS, LLC
THE GOLD STANDARD IN PUBLISHING

QUALITY BOOKS
IN BOTH PRINT AND ELECTRONIC FORMATS

ACTION/ADVENTURE	SUSPENSE/THRILLER
SCIENCE FICTION	DARK FANTASY
MAINSTREAM	ROMANCE
HORROR	EROTICA
FANTASY	GLBT
WESTERN	MYSTERY
PARANORMAL	HISTORICAL
YOUNG ADULT	NON-FICTION

AMBER QUILL PRESS, LLC
http://www.amberquill.com

Made in the USA
San Bernardino, CA
04 October 2013